# MURDER OVER EASY

*a Monona Quinn Mystery*

## MARSHALL COOK

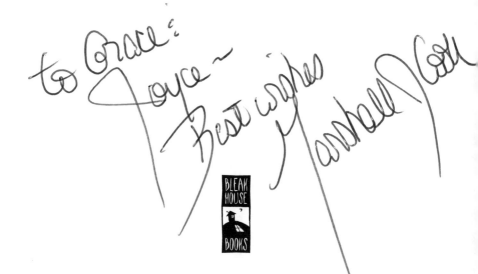

To Grace & Joyce ~
Best wishes
Marshall Cook

BLEAK HOUSE BOOKS

BLEAK HOUSE BOOKS
Published by Diversity Inc.

www.diversityincorporated.com

Diversity Inc.
P.O. Box 8573
Madison, WI 53708

This is a work of fiction. Any similarities to people or places, living or dead, is purely coincidental.

ISBN 0-9704098-6-9
Library of Congress Control Number:   2002116960

Jacket design: Peter Streicher
Book design: Jennifer Green
Cover photographs: Sharon Lomasney and Benjamin LeRoy

Text set in Baskerville

Printed in the United States of America

First Printing February 2003

*Dedicated to:*

*The publishers of those weekly miracles and
to the folks who make the hash browns and pour the coffee.*

# MURDER OVER EASY
*a Monona Quinn Mystery*

"What are you working on?"

"Who says I'm working on anything?" Monona Quinn glanced at her husband, elbow to elbow with her in her two-seater del Sol.

"You're not talking. That means you're either mad at me or you're working on something. I'm being optimistic."

She laughed. "Has the mystery gone out of our marriage?"

"Not a chance." He put his hand lightly on her knee.

She gripped the wheel tightly, leaning into the frequent bends in the country lane. The speedometer needle jiggled between 40 and 45, 15 to 20 miles above the posted limit.

"That's Wisconsin," he said. "The shortest distance between two points is 12 miles around somebody's farm. So. Which is it?"

"Which is what?"

"Are you mad at me, or are you working on something?"

"A little of one and a lot of the other," she admitted.

"It's not my fault we're late."

"True. But you were a pretty big pain in the butt about coming at all."

"Mo, I didn't even know the man. I mean, I'm sure he was a pillar of the community…"

"More like the foundation."

"Okay. The guy was a rock. I still didn't know him."

"I'm not sure I did, either."

"You had a lot of cups of coffee at that diner of his."

"You wouldn't get to know Charlie that way. He didn't talk much when he worked."

"You're taking his death hard."

Mo glanced at her husband, catching as she did a glimpse of the "Schuster's Sweet Swishers" barn mural. Still seven miles to Mitchell. She pressed down gently on the accelerator.

"I am," she admitted. "Charlie was the first one in town who made me feel welcome."

After eight months editing the weekly *Mitchell Doings*, Mo still felt like an outsider in the small, rural southcentral Wisconsin community. She had given up the excitement of Chicago and a column with the *Chicago Tribune* when she and Doug opted for country living. Mo often put in 80-hour weeks at the *Doings*, and Doug was pouring himself into trying to get his home-based investment counseling business going. That didn't leave much time for whatever social life Mitchell might offer.

She checked the speedometer. If she didn't get stuck behind a farmer jockeying a manure spreader from barn to field, they'd make it in time for the graveside part of the service, anyway.

"I don't think it was an accident," she said suddenly.

"Don't think what was an accident?"

"Charlie's death."

"Come on, Mo. He fell down the stairs. It happens. Isn't that what the Sheriff said?"

"Repoz is up for re-election in six months. He doesn't need another murder investigation to botch, after that Arnez business over in Two Creeks."

"That makes him self-interested, but it doesn't make him wrong."

"It doesn't make him right, either."

"Okay. Repoz has a .07 blood alcohol level. He's got head trauma and bruises consistent with a fall down the stairs. The stairs are steep, narrow, and poorly lit. There was no evidence of a break-in or a scuffle. What have you got?"

She smiled. That was Doug. Analytical. Play the cards straight up.

"Charlie got his .07 over at the VFW just about every night. That wouldn't have bothered him. The head trauma and bruises are also consistent with being bludgeoned with a blunt instrument. And Charlie's been negotiating those steps since he was 17 years old. He could do it in his sleep."

Doug considered all that. "Repoz still has you beat," he decided. "No suspect. No motive. You're dealing with a phantom killer."

"I've got a feeling."

"Oh, Lord," Doug said, rolling his eyes. "Nancy Drew's got a feeling."

"Don't patronize me, Douglas."

"I'm not."

She shot him a glance, the one he called The Look.

"Okay. I am. Was. I'm sorry. But listen, Mo. By your own accounts, this guy was as close to a saint as we're likely to see on earth. Who would want to whack him?"

Good point. If all Charlie had been to Mitchell was the guy who ran the diner, it would have been enough. Charlie's had been as close to a social center as a little town like

Mitchell had. Folks started gathering for coffee even before Charlie officially opened at 5, and he fed breakfast to just about everybody for miles around. His Everything-that-ain't-on-it-is-in-it Omelet, with a side of Potato Wreckage, was legendary.

But Charlie meant much more to Mitchell than good food and a gathering place. He'd been a member of the volunteer fire department since the day he turned 18, he was treasurer of the local co-op, a third-degree Mason, treasurer of the Lions, chair of the Fourth of July Fireworks Show, coordinator of the Fireman's Park Clean-Up crew, and vice-chair of the Messina Cemetery Association.

"Who would want to kill a man like that?" she said aloud.

"My point exactly."

"Point well taken."

"Maybe he keeled over from fatigue."

"At 43? With no history of illness?"

She saw the pickups and sedans lining both sides of the road ahead and eased off the accelerator, pulling over onto the shoulder to the staccato clatter of pebbles hitting the underside of the car.

"Looks like everybody in town turned out to plant Charlie proper," Doug said.

"Try not to get carried away with sentimentality."

"I'll try." He grinned at her as he unbuckled his seat belt—a precaution he took only when she drove, she had noticed.

They weren't the last ones to arrive. She heard a pickup grind through its downshift and skid to a stop behind them, heard the solid thwack of the door, heard a familiar voice call out, "Hey, folks. Wait up."

Andy Krueger was the owner of Krueger's Hardware and a regular at Charlie's mid-morning round table, where

Mitchell's movers and shakers downed endless cups of coffee, chewed over crops, prices, and local politics, and solved the world's problems.

"Good to see you, Mo, Douglas." Krueger was already sweating freely from his short shuffle to catch up to them, even in the crisp air of a late June morning. "You on duty, Mo, or just here as a civilian?"

"A reporter is always a reporter, Andy," Doug said, slapping the short, stocky man on one substantial shoulder.

She shot him The Look, but it struck only a glancing blow.

"Is that a fact?" A big grin spread over Krueger's broad face, exposing a gap between his two upper front teeth.

"Even when it's off the record, it's never off the record," Mo said, smiling at the notion of herself as intrepid investigative reporter.

They walked in silence, Mo on the shoulder, Doug to her left on the road, Krueger trailing. Mo could hear his wheezing. He needed to lose 50 pounds, she thought.

The cemetery was just ahead, sloping up to the left. It might just be the only cemetery in the world that overlooked an amusement park. But then, Mitchell had to be the only town with a population under 2,000 with its own amusement park for the cemetery to overlook.

Mourners fanned out 20 deep from Charlie's gravesite. Mo spotted Martha Adamski and her husband Horace, unofficial First Couple of Mitchell. Martha was President of the Town of Mitchell Counsel, and as owner/operators of Adamski's Supper Club, they were the most prominent business people in Mitchell. Adamski's was a local landmark, sitting three miles west of Mitchell, where the Oshnaube River bowed out to form a lake.

The Mitchell Caffeine Irregulars were standing together, in the same order they always sat along the counter at Charlie's. Put a mug of coffee in one hand and one of Charlie's chocolate-slathered donuts in the other, and they would have looked right at home.

The members of the Communal Crossword Puzzle Club were scattered throughout the crowd, paired off with husbands.

Mo realized with a start that she was trying to figure out which one of her neighbors was a murderer.

She also realized that she wasn't the only one. A short, thin young man was standing at the edge of the crowd, looking as inconspicuous as a stranger with a video camera at a funeral could look. He had to be a deputy sheriff, Mo figured, taping the funeral to try to pick up anybody who seemed out of place.

She spotted Dilly Nurtleman and wished she could talk to him. Of all the folks who depended on Charlie Connell, poor Dilly would probably miss him the most, would in fact be lost without him. Dilly had been hit by a car while riding his bike years before and had been "not quite right" ever since. But Charlie had discovered that Dilly could keep everybody's orders straight after hearing them once, without writing anything down, no matter how busy things got, and Dilly became a regular helper during the breakfast rush.

What would Dilly do without Charlie to take care of him—and, she realized, without Charlie to take care of?

For that matter, what would the town do without Charlie?

The VFW was well represented, and every member of the volunteer fire department was accounted for, along with most of Charlie's fellow parishioners of St. Anne's Catholic Church. By the time you got done figuring all Charlie's ties to the townsfolk, you'd counted everybody in town at least twice and sometimes three or four times.

But what did folks know about Charlie Connell's private

life? Did he even have a private life? And why couldn't Mo shake the feeling that he had been murdered?

Even Wallace J. Pierpont had come down from his sanctuary to attend services. Pierpont sightings were rare, unless you happened to catch him puttering with his trains or the roller coaster or bumper cars after the park had closed for the season, or maybe glimpsed him up by the house when you rode the miniature train out around the pond.

Thus employed taking mental inventory of the mourners, Mo took little note of Father O'Bannon's remarks. He was a gentle, caring pastor, tireless in serving his flock, but he was a dreadfully dull sermonizer. Mo had become accustomed to letting her mind wander while the priest droned on.

Soon enough it was time for food in the church basement—platters of substantial sandwiches of white bread with butter and mayo, a thick slice of Cheddar cheese and a thicker slab of glazed ham; bowls of three bean and seven layer salad; quivering Jell-O rings; tubs of German style potato salad.

Charlie's mother Charlene sat with quiet dignity at the table nearest the kitchen, flanked by what must have been Charlie's brothers. Mo guided Doug to the line that had formed to pass in review by the table, and when their turn came, she introduced them both to the first Connell brother.

"I'm Monona Quinn," she said, taking the stocky man's thick hand. "I edit the *Mitchell Doings*. This is my husband, Doug."

Brother Connell nodded. "The family surely does appreciate your turning out for Charlie's funeral," he said.

"We all thought the world of Charlie," Mo said. "I guess everybody's told you that."

But the Connell brother was already looking to the

next people in line, and Mo and Doug moved on to the food table, where they filled their paper plates with enough food to make a socially acceptable showing.

They settled in at a table across from Janice Pierce and Martha Bodine, two regular members of the Communal Crossword Club. Mo introduced them to Doug, who knew almost no one in the crowded basement.

"It's such a pleasure to meet you, Mr. Quinn," Martha Bodine gushed. "We've heard so much about you."

"It's Stennett, actually," Doug said, glancing at Mo.

"What's 'Stennett'?" Martha's face bunched in confusion.

"My name. My name is Stennett."

Martha looked from Doug to Mo and back to Doug. "Oh," she said, nodding, her mouth assuming the hint of a curl in one corner. "You two are shacking up, then."

Doug choked on a pickle embedded in the lime Jell-O.

"Let's vamoose," he hissed at Mo as soon as they had finished their food.

Mo nodded, getting to her feet. They had done their duty, and they both surely had plenty to do. Doug would already be organizing his afternoon's work in his mind, and she had a desk covered with correspondents' columns and readers' letters to edit, the news story on Charlie to finish, a few items to add to the 'Mo Knows' column that she accumulated rather than wrote each week, plus the latest developments in the growing school board controversy to try to verify.

Vera Nelson, the board's senior member and strongest advocate for "fiscal responsibility and family values" (to her supporters) or "mossback obstructionism" (to her detractors), was now claiming that Elmo Kastegen, her long-time antagonist on the board, had leaked the sealed bids on the new gymnasium to his brother-in-law in Madison, which would explain how the brother-in-law had managed to come in with a bid just under the previous low bid the day before the deadline.

But as soon as they got out into the cool early afternoon air, she knew she didn't want to drive home yet.

"Let's take a walk," she said, starting off down the highway, which in another hundred yards narrowed to become Main Street through the three blocks of businesses that comprised what folks in Mitchell meant when they said they were going 'downtown.'

"A walk?" He had to hurry to catch up to her. "Honey, I really have to get back…"

"I just want to take a look around at the diner," she said without looking back. "It won't take long."

"Nancy Drew, girl detective," he said.

But he kept walking with her into town, which looked like a deserted movie set waiting for the actors and crew to return from a break. There was the little diner at the cross-road, a dumpy two-story brick building with the "Charlie's Mitchell Diner" Coca Cola sign in front.

Yellow tape now cordoned off the diner. Mo raised the tape slightly as she ducked under, climbed the two steps, and rattled the front door knob. "Locked," she muttered.

"I believe they call this the scene of the crime," Doug said. "As in investigation. As in 'do not mess with.'"

But he trailed Mo to the side door, where a hand painted sign announced, "Enterence on Main Street." She reached out, not expecting the door to be unlocked, and recoiled slightly when it opened at her touch.

"Mo…"

"Come on. I just want to take a quick look."

"God help us."

"Ma'am?"

She whirled to see a uniformed deputy step from the shadows at the end of the building.

"I'm afraid you can't go in there."

"Told you," Doug muttered.

"I'm so sorry. I just wanted to take a look." Mo already had her card out and was extending it to the deputy, whose head appeared to be at least a size and a half too small for the broad-brimmed Sheriff's Department hat shading his upper face. "I'm Monona Quinn. I edit the *Mitchell Doings*. This is my husband, Douglas Stennett. He's a financial advisor."

"Yes, ma'am," the deputy said, glancing at the card before pushing up the starched flap of his shirt pocket and shoving the card in.

"I'm also…was also a friend of the deceased."

"You and everybody else in town," the deputy said, pursing his lips and nodding.

"Well," Mo said. "We'll be getting along, then."

"Yes, ma'am." The deputy appeared relieved.

"Would you be sure to have someone give me a call if you have anything I might be able to use in my newspaper?"

"Yes, ma'am."

"Perhaps we could sit down after this is all over, and I could do a feature on you. What it's like to work for a big county sheriff's department. Some of the cases you've solved. That sort of thing. My readers would find it fascinating."

The deputy's cheeks turned pink. "I'm not so sure about that," he said.

When they were again on the legal side of the police barrier, Doug put his arm around his wife's shoulders and drew her to him. "Oh, brother," he hissed as they walked out of the deputy's earshot. "You laid it on pretty thick."

"They're treating the diner as a crime scene. They even posted a guard at the door."

"I'm sure that's just routine."

"I don't think so."

"Too bad you couldn't snoop around, Nancy Drew. You might have picked up some clues."

"Who says I didn't?"

They nodded to a line of folks walking back to town from the church. When they were again alone, Doug said, "What are you talking about? You didn't even get in the door."

"But I saw through the door and down the stairs."

"And saw what? A signed confession hanging on the railing?"

"Nope. Clean, starched aprons hanging neatly from their hooks on the wall."

"That's a clue?"

She fished out her car key and fumbled it into the driver's side door lock. Then she met his gaze over the top of the car. A minivan whooshed by. Andy Krueger's truck was still parked behind them.

"If you started to fall down the steps, what would you do?"

He thought about that. "Try to stop myself," he said.

"How?"

He shrugged. Then awareness spread across his face. "I'd try to grab hold of something," he said softly.

"Bingo. And you'd take at least a couple of aprons down with you."

She opened her door, clicked his door unlocked, and they slid into their bucket seats.

"Doesn't prove a thing," he insisted.

"Nope," she admitted, pressing down on the accelerator. "It doesn't."

"But you still think Charlie Connell was murdered."

"You bet I do."

Gravel flew up behind them as Mo charged back onto the road.

*The man gropes in the dim light. Darkness hovers above him, a shadow within shadows. She knows beyond knowing that this shadow means to kill the groping man.*

*She tries to scream but can make no sound. She floats between the man and the darkness.*

*The man reaches the base of the stairway and starts to drag himself up, the thudding of his feet echoing in the darkness. He moans.*

*The darkness expands to fill the space between itself and the man on the staircase. When it touches the man, it will destroy him. She knows this. A low animal moaning shivers her as the man labors up the stairs, the evil swelling to envelop him.*

"Mo? Honey? What is it?"

Her eyes opened. She struggled to sit up, beating the covers away as if they were stinging her.

"You were having a nightmare."

He tried to hold her, but she gathered into herself, hunching forward and twisting away from him, and hugged her knees to her chest.

"That must have been a humdinger." His hand was light on her shoulder, tentative, questioning.

"I don't remember what happened. I just remember the feeling."

"What did you feel?"

"Death."

"Oh, honey."

"Not mine. I was watching."

"Who was it?"

She tried to bring the dream back and couldn't and was glad. She shook her head, feeling his arm slide around her shoulder and draw her to him.

"Why do our minds do that to us?" he said softly, stroking her back and gently massaging her neck.

She could barely feel her pulse throbbing in her throat now. She craned her neck to see the digital clock on the nightstand. It showed 5:42, almost time to get up.

He squeezed her shoulder. She turned and curled into his embrace.

"I hope what we did last night didn't give you nightmares."

"You know better."

He smiled at the memory. She rubbed his stubbly cheek and remembered. He had been cranky about having to go to the funeral. They ate dinner in silence, and he fell asleep in his recliner, a sheaf of papers spread out in his lap. It seemed all he could do to drag himself upstairs, shrug out of his clothes, and fall into bed.

Certain from his heavy, regular breathing that he had already fallen asleep, she had clicked off the television and the bedside light, and Jack Roosevelt had settled into his spot behind the crook of her knees and started purring himself to sleep. She was herself already drifting toward sleep when she felt his hand gently patting her shoulder, posing its question.

Apparently he wasn't cranky or tired any more.

She took his hand and put it on her breast. He cupped her, squeezing gently, a finger gently rubbing her nipple under the flannel nightgown. His other hand found her belly, rubbing gently, sliding down between her legs.

Not one bit cranky or tired.

They had made love gently, with the ease of long practice and mutual knowledge. She was ready for him when he thrust into her, pushing her pelvis up to accept him deeply. She heard him gasp, then sigh, felt his jagged breath against her face.

The lovemaking felt comfortable and right. Doug built eagerly to his climax, one hand tightening on the back of her neck, the other rushing through her hair and pushing her head back gently.

He moaned as he came, fighting his arms around her and crushing her to him. His body relaxed. She felt his heavy, rapid breathing, so that it was hard to tell where his breathing left off and her own began.

He had rolled over and fell almost immediately to sleep, but sleep had been elusive for Mo.

Then Doug was waking her from her nightmare.

She pushed the covers off, slipped her legs over the edge of the bed and pivoted to a sitting position.

"Getting up?"

"Yeah. You go back to sleep. You've still got 40 minutes."

"Okay."

She pulled on her robe. Jack Roosevelt would stay up with Doug until she'd had her first mug of coffee. For an instant the feeling of the dream returned, and she felt herself tense. The feeling passed through her. Shivering, she padded downstairs into the kitchen, got the coffee perking, pulled the Madison paper off the side porch, and brought Doug's *Wall Street Journal* in from the front lawn.

She paged rapidly through the front section. Charlie was front page, upper right in the local section. Lee Mayer's clean, crisp prose described the line that ringed McKendrick's Funeral Home for four hours during the vigil two nights ago and the throng at the church and the graveside yesterday. He noted the presence of a Dane County Sheriff videotaping the services.

Mayer covered cops and courts for the Madison *Cardinal-Herald* and generally did a fine job—when he wasn't too distracted trying to write his true crime books. She idly wondered if he was planning to write one about Charlie. His presence on the story indicated that city editor Charles Dutton must figure Charlie for a homicide.

She scanned the birth announcements and obits and flipped to the sports section to check out the box scores. Mo was a diehard Cubs fan (was there any other kind?), a lifelong affliction her husband's gentle teasing had done nothing to lessen.

She heard Doug's footfalls overhead, followed by the scrape and thunk of the bathroom door. He hadn't been able to get back to sleep either. A moment later, she heard the water pound against the shower stall.

"Some enchanted evening," Doug's careless baritone floated downstairs. She smiled. He was still in a good mood from last night.

The coffee pot wasn't yet full, but she pulled it out from its cradle and poured a mug quickly, the spillage sizzling as it hit the hot plate.

Jack Roosevelt weaved around her legs, almost tripping her.

"Hold your horses, Jackie boy old buddy," she said as

she fetched the kibble bin from the cupboard and filled his bowl. Jack Roosevelt began purring the moment the bin came out and didn't stop as he began to eat.

That boy likes his breakfast, she thought as she took her coffee cup and the sports section into the bathroom, where she read the Cubs box score—another Cub loss, despite Sammy Sosa's two-run home run, and pulled on her sweats. Then she went into the den and popped an exercise tape into the VCR.

"Okay, Janie baby," she challenged the flickering image on the screen. "Do your worst. I'm ready for you this morning."

She panted through her workout, took her shower, dressed and returned to the kitchen, where Jack Roosevelt was staring at his water bowl. Doug had taken his *Wall Street Journal* and his coffee mug and was no doubt at the computer terminal in his office.

Jack Roosevelt continued to stare at the nearly full bowl. She got the jug of distilled water from the broom closet and filled the bowl with fresh water. "Sure you wouldn't like a twist of lemon with that?" she asked him.

She grabbed a poppy seed bagel and smeared it with cream cheese lite. "I'm heading out," she called.

"Where to so early?"

"Cora Beth Watkins. Remember?"

"Right. Hold on."

He stepped out of his office, cupped her head in his hands, and gave her a long, tender kiss.

"What time will you be home, lover?"

"I have to finish Charlie's obit. And the column. And proof the correspondence. And..."

"I'll make chicken."

"That would be nice. But you should make some calls. Business won't just come walking through the door."

"Thanks, boss."

"I didn't mean to nag."

"I know."

She guided the car out of town and onto the gentle rises and dips of County YY, one of the many farm roads linking the little towns and giving dairy farmers a way to get their milk to market every morning. Winter refused to let loose this year, she reflected, looking at the bleak fields, where patches of snow still clung to the low spots.

She thought about how sad Doug had looked, standing in the doorway watching her pull away. He was having such a hard time trying to sell himself. He was by nature very shy and would be content to sit at his computer all day. She had left his card when she made the rounds with the advertising salesman she had inherited from the previous editor.

Despite this worry and the lingering sorrow from yesterday's funeral, Mo was looking forward to talking with Cora Beth Watkins again. Cora Beth had been confined to her home with crippling arthritis, with only Minnie, her miniature schnauzer, for company for the eight years since her husband died. Her house sat only a couple hundred yards from where the train derailed with its potentially lethal load of propane, and she had been among the first to be evacuated. When the National Guard came for her, Minnie sat at the foot of the basement steps Cora Beth could no longer climb, yapping furiously at the intrusion. There was no time to round up pets, the boyish Guardsman had told her. The propane could blow any minute.

A Sun Prairie family, the McCarty's, gave Cora Beth their spare room, where she wept for three days, sure her precious Minnie would die.

Then had come the Mysterious Stranger. Mo wanted to know more about that mysterious stranger.

Minnie greeted Mo's arrival with desperate enthusiasm.

"She'll quiet down in a moment," Cora Beth assured her, clutching her walker with two hands after wrestling the door open. "Minnie! You behave!"

Minnie had no intention of behaving but did in fact settle down to some serious pants sniffing, picking up essence of Jack Roosevelt. At Cora Beth's urging, Mo sank into the tattered couch. Minnie jumped into her lap and licked her face.

"I guess I pass inspection," Mo said with a laugh.

"She's a naughty little girl," Cora Beth said, maneuvering herself into position to plop into the overstuffed armchair that was the only other sitting place in the room.

Mo found herself scanning an array of photographs, figurines of birds suspended in flight from plastic mounts, doilies, candle holders—none of them holding candles—a metronome, two empty vases, and a stack of photo albums. Every inch of horizontal space was covered at least once. The framed photographs all appeared to be of the same couple, at various ages—Cora Beth and her dear departed husband, Elbert. The room could have been a shrine to their marriage.

"I'm a member of the Bird of the Month Club," Cora Beth announced proudly. "That's a cardinal you're looking at there. Isn't it beautiful? Every month I get a new one. I used to keep birds, real ones, I mean, but that was when I could still get around, of course."

Cora Beth was off and running. She had apparently been saving up human conversation for some time. Mo needed only to guide Cora Beth to the Saga of the Mysterious Stranger.

"He just appeared at the door of the McCarty's one night and said he'd get my Minnie for me."

"Did you recognize him?"

"No. But I don't know a lot of the young folks from

town any more. He had an orange stocking cap. I remember that. He said he'd sneak past the police line and save my Minnie for me."

The protagonist of the story wriggled away from Mo, jumped up next to Cora Beth, put her muzzle on her mistress's lap and heaved a sigh.

"How did he get into your house?"

"Why, I gave him the key, of course."

"That didn't worry you?"

"No," Cora Beth said slowly, as if confused. "He seemed like a nice, trustworthy young man." Then she brightened. "Didn't Jim McCarty read me out when I told him what I'd done, though? Said I might just as well have put all my things out in the street with a sign saying 'Steal Me.' It was all I could do to keep him from calling the police."

"What happened then?"

"Why, everybody went to bed, and I fell asleep in the recliner chair in the living room. I heard a scratching, and when I opened my eyes, there was Minnie, big as life, looking at me through the window.

"The young man said Minnie hadn't wanted to come with him, but he'd lured her using some dog biscuits he had in his pocket. Minnie just licked me and licked me and raced around the house, barking until she woke everybody up!"

Minnie roused herself enough to wag her hind end and lick her mistress's hand.

"And wasn't that Jim McCarty surprised!" Cora Beth said happily. Then her face turned serious. "I wanted to give that young man something for all his trouble," she said, frowning. "But by the time everything got settled down, he'd gone off without a by-your-leave. Imagine that."

"You refer to him as a 'young man,'" Mo asked. "About how old do you think he was?"

"Oh, he could have been 16, I suppose," Cora Beth said. "Of course, they all look young when you get to my age. He could have been older than that, I suppose. It was hard to see his face. He wore that old stocking cap, and the collar of his jacket was pulled up all the way around. It was down around five above that night, as I recollect. And he never stayed long enough to unwrap. I wanted to offer him a cup of cocoa—the poor thing seemed near frozen—but then I remembered that I wasn't in my own home, and I didn't want to trouble that nice Mrs. McCarty."

"And you have no idea who he is or where he lives?"

Minnie roused, jumped down from the chair, and popped up next to Mo on the couch, dropping a yellow rubber mouse in her lap. Minnie yipped, her eyes on Mo's face, and snatched up the mouse again.

"Noooooooo. I can't say that I do. And I never have seen him since. I'd sure like to give him a reward, not money, of course. I haven't got anything but dear Elbert's Social Security, and that doesn't stretch very far, but I could knit him a new stocking cap or bake him a batch of my chocolate chip walnut cookies."

They got tangled up in Cora Beth's special recipe for chocolate chip walnut cookies—the secret was apparently in the obscene amount of real butter she used. Mo folded her hands in her lap, trying to keep her right leg from shaking with impatience.

Mo wanted that Mysterious Stranger. He would make the story.

"Is there anything else you can remember about him?" she prompted when Cora Beth ran out of breath.

"Noooooooo. Wait, now!"

Mo's heart jumped.

"No. That's the boy who comes to collect for the newspaper."

Mo gathered up her coat and gloves.

"Do you have to go so soon?"

"I'm afraid I do," Mo said. "No, no," she added quickly, seeing Cora Beth reaching for her walker and beginning to struggle up out of the chair. "Please don't get up. Just let me get a couple of pictures of you and Minnie."

"Oh, merciful heavens," Cora Beth said, her hand flying up to pat at her hair. "I look a fright! And Minnie needs her little face washed."

Even so, Cora Beth beamed while Mo snapped a dozen shots with Minnie squirming in her lap.

Mo pressed a card into the elderly woman's hand. "Will you give me a call if you remember anything else about that young hero of yours? I'd surely love to talk to him."

"Well, so would I," Cora Beth said earnestly. "I'm sure he'd love a batch of those cookies."

"I'm sure he would." Mo high stepped over and around Minnie to reach the front door.

"Do come again," Cora Beth called after her.

Mo hoped she could. Cora Beth was a sweet woman, with lots of stories to tell. Mo slid in behind the wheel and flipped open her notebook to jot down some of the details of Cora Beth's nearly nonstop monologue. She had enough for 600 words, with a three-column photo of Cora Beth with Minnie, but it would pretty much be a rehash of the story she'd written at the time of the derailment.

Mo soon forgot about Cora Beth, Minnie, and the Mysterious Stranger as she got caught up in the rush of the day. Editing a community weekly was not for the faint of heart, and Mondays tended to be second only to Tuesdays for long hours and chaos.

Doug had the table set and the chicken baking when she finally straggled home.

"Any messages?" she asked when they had exchanged a kiss.

"Nope. I had an interesting call, though."

"Who from?"

"Andy Krueger. He wants to talk to me about expanding his business. Needs some financial planning advice."

"That's wonderful."

"You wouldn't have had anything to do with it, would you?"

"I gave him your card. Weeks ago. I'm sure it was seeing you at the funeral yesterday."

"I know. Networking. Well, anyway..." He held out a package, wrapped in the Sunday comic section.

"What's this?"

He grinned like a little boy caught in unexpected goodness. "It's nothing, really," he said quickly, watching her face.

"What did you do?" She hefted it tentatively. The paper gave slightly along one side, a dead giveaway. Surely a book.

"You could probably take it out to County General and get them to X-ray it for you," Doug said. "Or you could do something really crazy, like maybe, oh, I don't know, open it!"

He was rip. She was savor. But this time she ripped.

"Oh, Dougie. Where ever did you find this?"

"I hunted all over State Street. Paul's didn't have it, and neither did Shakespeare's. I was about to give up, but there was this one little store that I don't think was even there the last time we were in Madison."

"I told you I read them when I was a girl. And you remembered!"

She smiled down at the cover, familiar after all the years. "NANCY DREW MYSTERY STORIES" was printed in yellow across the top of the cover and then, in white type centered against the dark, cloudy night sky, the title in capital letters: "THE SECRET OF THE OLD CLOCK. "

Nancy Drew was sitting in the grass, her legs tucked up under her. In her left hand she held a screwdriver, and her right hand supported a table clock. The glass door of the clock was open, exposing the dial. The clock showed 18 minutes before 2 o'clock.

The words "by Carolyn Keene" were tucked down in the lower left part of the cover. It could have been the very copy she had as a girl. But that was silly. What were the odds of such a thing?

She leafed to the cover page, which repeated the title and author and announced the publisher to be Grosset & Dunlap, New York. As she read the words, she noted a musty, damp odor. This book had sat in somebody's basement, without benefit of dehumidifier, through many Wisconsin summers.

And with the dank essence came the memory of a man groping in darkness, an evil presence hovering over him. She gasped and sank into her chair.

"Mo! What's the matter?"

"I started to remember my nightmare."

He took the book from her and enveloped her hands in his. "Tell me. Can you?"

"Nothing to tell. Really. It was just black and threatening. Somebody—or something—about to hurt somebody."

"Is that all you remember?"

She nodded. He squeezed her hands.

"I know you don't put any stock in such things, but I really think the dream is telling me something."

"Like what?"

"That someone murdered Charlie Connell."

"I was in the diner one time when the siren went off," Horace Adamski said. He was dipping soapy glasses in the rinse sink and setting them upside down on cloth towels on the bar to dry. "Hope you don't mind if I keep working while we talk," he said.

"Not a bit," Mo said from her perch on the stool at the end of the bar. She could see into the dining room, where Martha Adamski was folding cloth napkins into cones and placing one at each setting at the banquet table.

"Old Charlie was out from behind the counter before the first wail of the siren died down," Horace continued, smiling at the memory. "He had his apron off and was out the door before it started up the second time.

"This was mid-morning, mind you, and Charlie was handling the place all by himself. But he didn't hesitate. Just told folks to help themselves to what they needed and leave the money by the register."

The rinsing and setting of glasses had slowed to a near halt.

"He risked his neck time and time again for his neighbors. One time he went back into a burning building to get

Mable Matusak's quilt that had won her a blue ribbon at the County Fair.

"Joined up the day he turned 18. Charlie couldn't wait. You see that old toy fire truck he had on that shelf above the grill? The boys gave him that after he got 10 years in. It was a way to tell him what a hell of a job he was doing."

"Keep working on those glasses, Mister," Martha said, bustling through on her way to the kitchen. "We got the Rotary in less than two hours."

Horace smiled after his wife as she disappeared through the swinging doors but made no move on the glasses.

"What else can I tell you? He wasn't just a pillar of this community. He was all four corners and the roof. Chaired the Fourth of July Fireworks, coordinated the Fireman's Park Clean-Up every spring, made sure everything got done for the big parade."

Mo looked up from her notepad when the voice didn't resume. Horace was standing, hands at his sides, chin down.

"Hell's bells," he said softly. He might have been talking to himself. "We got that parade in another two weeks. I don't know how we're going to pull it off without him." Horace cleared his throat, rousing himself. "Folks say there's nobody that's indispensable," he said, looking at Mo. "But those folks never met Charlie Connell."

Mo braced herself. "Did you know of anybody who might have wanted to hurt him?" she asked.

Horace snorted, the left corner of his mouth curling up in what on a less friendly face would have been a sneer. "That fool County Mountie asked me that, too," he said, shaking his head. "Little sawed-off fella. Banty rooster type. I felt like popping him one." He looked at Mo, what would have been a sneer turning back into the broad, guileless smile. "I'll tell you the same thing I told him, same as I'd tell anybody. Charlie Connell didn't have an enemy in this town. Wasn't nobody didn't think the world of Charlie Connell."

"He never married?"

"Charlie? No. He always said no woman would have him. Couldn't keep up with him was more like it. Nope. Never married or anything, as far as anybody knows." He winked. "But then," he added, "even small town folk have their secrets. He might have had a lady in Madison."

"What makes you say that?"

"Oh, nothing, really. He'd go off to Madison sometimes on a Saturday, after he'd closed up the diner, and his car would still be gone Sunday morning."

"And you think he went to visit a lady friend?"

"I didn't say that."

"Horace! I need you in the kitchen!"

He grinned and shrugged. "My master's voice." The grin faded. "I have no idea who he might have been visiting," he said. "I don't know that he was visiting anybody. Isn't that something? I seen him just about every day for the last I don't know how many years, but I guess I didn't know all that much about him after all."

"Who else should I talk to?" Mo said, tucking her pencil into the spiral binding of her notebook.

Horace thought about that. "Talk to the gals that worked for him, of course," he said. "Charlie's Angels, they called themselves. And Dilly, of course. Dilly followed that man around like somebody's old dog."

"Anybody else?"

"I guess Norb Hopkins knew Charlie as good as anybody."

"The wrestling coach?"

"Sure. Charlie used to help out with practices and meets and such."

"Charlie was a wrestler?"

"He look like a wrestler to you?"

"No."

"I guess he just loved the sport. I think he and Norb was pretty good buddies. And you know Charlie. Always helping out anybody who needed helping."

. . . .

"I'm thinking of starting a second business, and I wanted to get some feedback on how I might finance the deal."

Andy Krueger led Doug through the narrow aisle of the cluttered hardware store to the back and down the basement steps to a tiny office carved out of mounds of inventory that hadn't made it to the ground floor yet. The basement was a good 20 degrees cooler than the upstairs.

"To tell you the truth, I'm not sure I can swing it without getting in way over my head," Andy admitted. "I figured that might be right up your alley."

"You can just put all that crap on the floor. Anyplace is fine. Careful. That chair's got a lot of give to it."

Doug sank into the battered old wing chair. Andy took the highback swivel chair behind the desk.

"Mo said you'd be able to help me," Andy said.

"Did she?" Doug tried not to sound excited at the prospect of getting a local client. He had built his consulting business largely on old Chicago contacts, and most of that business was beginning to dry up now that he was so far from the city.

"She's your number one booster, that little lady."

Doug smiled. "What kind of business do you want to start?" he asked.

"Not start. I'm too old for that. I want to take over an existing business."

"Good. You've got past performance to look at."

"Right. This business seems real solid."

"Here in town?"

"Yep. Right here in town."

"And the owner's willing to sell?"

Andy shifted his bulk in the chair and leaned forward. He collected loose papers from the desk and tried to neaten them into a pile. "The owner's dead," he said. "It was Charlie. I'm thinking of trying to buy the diner. I guess it goes to his brothers now."

Andy tossed the papers back on the desk. "I feel pretty damn funny about it," he said. "Charlie hardly cold in his grave and all. But I figure this town needs that diner. Without it, we're not really a community. If I can get it up and running real quick like, why, folks won't get out of the habit of coming in. And I could keep the same staff. She'd run smooth from day one. Except I'd have to hire somebody to cook, of course."

"And you want me to check out the business for you?"

"Yeah. That past performance we were talking about. Find out who owns it. If everything looks good to you, we can talk about how I could swing the deal."

Doug leaned back, almost lost in the deep, soft cushion. "I could get some information together for you. We could discuss how you wanted to proceed from there."

"That would be fan-damn-tastic!" Andy seemed to relax for the first time. "Like I said, I feel a little funny about this. Though there's no reason why I should, really, you think about it. I'm the last guy in the world would have wanted to see Charlie dead. But he is dead, and that diner's just going to sit there empty, and, well, like they say, business is business. Right?"

"Absolutely," Doug said. "Business is definitely business."

. . . .

"I feel almost slimy," Doug admitted that night after he reported his conversation with Andy Krueger to Mo over dinner on the screened-in back porch.

"Why?"

Doug speared several carrot dollars and forked them into his mouth. "It's like picking through a dead man's belongings," he said.

"Andy's right about the town needing the diner."

"And Lord knows, I need every client I can get. But it still bothers me."

"Speaking of clients, Dan Weilman would like to make an appointment with you."

"Weilman?"

"He owns the video rental across the street from the diner. He wants help getting his inventory computerized."

"So he called a financial consultant?"

"You can do that kind of thing in your sleep."

"But how does this Weilman know that?"

Mo got busy with her mashed potatoes. Doug waited her out.

"I might have mentioned it," she said when she ran out of mashed potatoes to play with.

"Mentioned it."

"Networking."

"I hate that word."

"I know you do, Douglas. That's why I end up having to do it for you."

Doug paused, a forkful of potatoes halfway to his mouth.

"I didn't mean that the way it sounded," Mo said.

"That's okay. You're probably right."

"It isn't a matter of who's right. I just want to help."

"I know you do."

An unhappy silence settled over them, broken only by the sound of Jack Roosevelt nosing his food bowl across the tile floor in the kitchen. Doug cleared the plates and brought out coffee.

"I've got to call the high school wrestling coach and set up an interview for tomorrow, if I can," she said while he poured.

"You taking wrestling lessons along with the karate now?"

"Very funny. Horace Adamski says the coach knew Charlie about as well as anybody in town."

"Be careful. Those wrestlers know all the holds."

"I'm not training with the Amazon lady of Madison for nothing. I can handle a smelly old wrestling coach."

"You sure? About the coach being smelly and old?"

"I don't think I've ever seen him, actually. I did interview one of his athletes, though. In another context, some sort of student council deal. You will follow up with Weilman, won't you?"

"I will. All by myself."

"Could you ask him about Charlie for me? I'll never have a chance to interview everybody I should for this story."

"What do you want me to ask him?"

"Just see if you can pick up anything interesting."

"For the story?"

"Of course for the story."

"You're not looking for clues, then?"

"Clues?"

"As in murder."

"I'm after information. I run a newspaper, remember?"

"I remember. I just wanted to make sure you did."

"Let me tell you something about Charlie Connell," Norbert Hopkins said, hunkering forward in his chair and putting his fists side by side on his desk. "There wasn't a better man alive. A better man never drew breath. You put that in your story, Missy. And you put in there that I said so."

"He was on your wrestling team?" Mo sat across a desk heaped with the debris of Norbert Hopkins' 42 years as coach, athletic director, and health ed teacher at Mitchell High School. Amidst the folders and programs and gum wrappers and bags that once held take-out from the DQ and still retained the grease, Mo was fairly certain she saw a jock strap.

Hopkins nodded vigorously, his jaws working a mouthful of sunflower seeds. "He started out as student manager. Best one I ever had. Like my right-hand man. I'd no sooner think a thing, and he'd have it done. Equipment laid out, mats cleaned and rolled up, towels for the shower room, anything. That was right when I took over as athletic director, too. I don't know how I would of done it all without Charlie."

"That would have been, what, 20 years ago?"

Coach leaned over to spit seed husks into the metal wastebasket by the desk. "He was a freshman the year we went to the Class D State Semi's. That would have been…" He stared off into space. "Nineteen seventy-eight," he decided.

Mo nodded, casually flipping open her pad and noting the year. She tried not to grimace as Hopkins elaborately cracked his knuckles.

"And he went right on helping out with the teams after he graduated, kind of like an assistant coach, but strictly volunteer. He even helped drive the kids to the away meets after they cancelled the bus service, busy as he was with the diner and all."

"Didn't he want to be on the team?"

"How's that?"

"Didn't Charlie want to be a member of the team instead of just being the manager?"

"He was a member of the team. The manager lettered, same as everybody else."

"But didn't he want to compete?"

For a bad moment, Mo was afraid the Coach intended to fire his 10-knuckle salute again. Instead, he clasped his hands and turned them out, palms toward Mo, as if warding her off.

"I don't know as he did, to be perfectly honest with you. He figured he could make a bigger contribution by helping everybody else do his best. That was Charlie down to the ground."

"Did he try out for the team?"

The chair squeaked as he shifted his bulk. "Yep. Three years out of the four."

"He wasn't good enough?"

"Wasn't big enough." More leaning and spitting. Seed husks spattered the floor.

"You have weight classifications, don't you?"

The scowl intensified. The Coach heaved a sigh. "Yep," he said. "We have weight classifications. Charlie just wasn't quick enough to wrestle small, and he couldn't keep the weight on to wrestle big.

"Fact is, Charlie just didn't have that killer instinct. He wanted to compete, but he just didn't have the stomach for hurting anybody. But he had the biggest heart on the team. I told them that, with Charlie standing right there in the locker room. I told 'em, 'if the rest of you fellas had a heart the size of this young man here, we'd be state champs.' That's the God's truth, Missy. You should put that in your story, too."

Mo let the silence gather between them.

"He made his contribution," the Coach said. "Just like he always did for this town."

"Why didn't he try out the fourth year?"

The Coach tipped back in his chair and examined the water stains on the ceiling. "I believe he'd already bought the diner his senior year."

"How did he manage to do that?"

"Worked his ass off. Saved every penny. Borrowed some money from his mama, I heard."

Mo scribbled on her pad. "Who else should I talk to about him?" she asked. "Did he have any friends?"

"He had a hell of a lot of friends! Hell, everybody in this town was his friend!"

"How about women friends?"

Coach leaned back, hooking his thumbs in the elastic band of his sweat pants. "You writing this for the *Doings* or the *National Enquirer*?"

Mo smiled. "The *Doings*," she assured him.

"You talk to the gals that worked with him. Talk to Sabra Farnum. She'll tell you what kind of man Charlie was."

"Coach?"

A short, wiry young man stood in the doorway.

"Yeah?"

"That guy's here with the new mats. He says you've got a check for him."

"Hold on." The chair protested as the coach shoved to his feet. "This lady was just leaving."

"Hello," Mo said. "You're Marcus, right?"

"Yes," the young man said.

"Mo Quinn." She offered him her hand for shaking. "I interviewed you for an article on student government."

"Right."

"You were student body vice president, weren't you?"

"Yes, ma'am."

"He'll be president this year," coach offered, coming out from behind the desk and positioning himself between Marcus and Mo. "And he's 35-3 in his weight class."

"Very impressive," Mo said. "What about enemies? Did Charlie have any enemies?"

"You talk to Sabra. Ask her about that skuzzy little mutt Charlie took in six months ago."

"Charlie had a dog?"

The coach snorted. "A derelict kid. Helped out around the diner, supposedly. Skinny little vagrant. About Marcus's height, but no muscle development whatsoever."

"Coach? That guy is waiting."

"Are we done?" Coach asked Mo.

"For now," Mo said.

She had the feeling they were both glad to see her leave.

. . . .

"Charlie was a hell of a guy," Dan Weilman allowed, "but he wasn't no kind of a business man."

Weilman owned and operated Starlite Video Movie Rental, next to Sylvia's Hair Apparent and just across Main Street from Charlie's.

"That's no knock on Charlie," Weilman added quickly. He was sitting in a ratty director's chair behind the counter. He would have had to stand to see over the counter.

The bell over the door tinkled behind Doug, who stood in front of the counter, attaché in hand. He'd worried about how he'd work the conversation around to Charlie after they talked business, but Dan was making it easy for him.

"Two at a time, fellas," Dan said. "You know the rules."

Doug turned to see three gangly male adolescents filling what Dan called the lobby.

"Ah, come on, Wild Man," one protested. He seemed to have the most twitches, the most insolent smirk, and the worst outbreak of acne—traits that perhaps qualified him to be the spokesperson. "We won't mess up your precious videos. Besides, you let Mary Lou Fenner in here with her bunch the other day. I seen 'em in here."

"You want to look at my videos, you abide by my rules."

"Geez. It ain't like you ever actually get any new flicks in here."

"I got the new Van Damme, Miley," Dan said, raising his eyebrows and smiling broadly.

When they filmed the story of Dan Weilman's life, Doug decided, they'd cast Danny De Vito in the lead.

"Wait here, Dweeb-o," Miley directed one of his cohorts.

"No way," Dweeb-o protested.

"Way."

"I'm gonna split, then."

"So, split." Miley and his remaining sidekick passed through the scanner and into the 'theater,' where videos were shelved by "Action/adventure," "Comedy," "Classics," "Horror/sci fi," "Children's/cartoons," and "The Wild Man's Golden Oldies."

Dan watched as they disappeared behind the first row before turning back to Doug. "Never rent a thing," he said, shaking his head.

"You were talking about Charlie being a bad business man."

"Yeah, yeah, yeah." Dan folded his hands over his gut and leaned back in the director's chair. "He was a hard worker. Make no mistake about that. That man put in the hours. If anything, he spread himself too thin, what with all the other projects he had going."

Dan put his hand in his mouth and began gnawing on the first knuckle of the index finger, making his next words hard to understand.

"The problem was, he was just too soft a touch. Need something done, ask Charlie. Somebody come to the back door and put the touch on him, old Charlie would make him up a sandwich and give him a bag of chips and a bottle of beer. Some of the regulars been running a tab for about as long as the diner's been open.

He finished gnawing down the knuckle.

"Let me put it to you this way. Somebody don't pay for their subscription, your wife don't keep delivering the newspaper. Am I right? That's just common sense."

Doug nodded.

"Cash and carry, brother. That's the only way to run a business."

Adolescent male laughter tumbled out from the back of the store.

"Get outta the adult material," Dan yelled without turning his head, "or I'll throw your shaggy asses out of here."

"Was Charlie having money problems?"

Dan's bushy black eyebrows shot up in surprise. "Not Charlie. Fact is, he'd paid off the paper on the diner and was free and clear. Of course, it was his mama holding the note, so he got a pretty good interest rate, shall we say."

Dan leaned so far back in the chair, he seemed to be defying gravity. "The way I heard it, they had it laid out as a 20-year loan," he said, "but Charlie paid it off in under 10."

"A very conservative approach."

Dan scowled. "Conservative!" He leaned forward, the front legs of the director's chair smacking the concrete floor. "Stupid, I'd call it. You structure the loan as a mortgage, and let the old lady take her interest on it. She can always kick it back to him under the table if she wants to. But you take the interest off your taxes anyway, right? About the only deduction the goverment still allows the little guy. You take the full 20 years to pay it off, getting your deduction every year. That would of been good business."

A bubble of stifled laughter surfaced from the back.

"That's it!" Dan shouted. "You're outta here!"

He turned back to Doug. "Ain't it? Good business, I mean? You're the expert."

"That would depend," Doug said.

"Depend on what?"

"On what you did with the money you would have used to pay down the loan faster."

A grin spread over Dan's jowly face. "That's where you come in, right? Say I wanted to borrow on the equity of my store, here, take my tax deduction on the interest, and invest the dough in something that would pay me twice what I'm paying in interest."

"You could do that," Doug said. "What would you want to invest in?"

"You tell me. What's good?

"How much? And for how long?"

"$20,000, say. And I could leave it awhile."

For only the second time since the move from Chicago, Doug felt himself on solid footing with one of his new neighbors, talking a language he understood, as he outlined various investment options.

When Doug finished, Dan pushed up out of the director's chair and stuck a pudgy hand over the counter for Doug to shake. "You write up your recommendations for me, bro," he said, "and get back to me. We'll do this thing. And I still want you to show me what software to use to computerize my inventory."

"Great."

"And tell your wife to write the hell out of her story on Charlie, will you? He deserves it. Hell of a guy. Just no businessman."

"I will."

"Tell her to come talk to me. I can tell her some things she don't know about Charlie."

"I'll tell her."

"All right!" Dan hollered, waddling toward the rear of the store. "Prepare to get your sorry carcasses hauled outta here!"

Doug showed himself out, eager to get home and write up his report for his new client.

# 5

Good, Doug thought as he eased the CR-V in at their gate and up the winding drive. Mo's del Sol wasn't perched by the front deck where she always left it in good weather. He should have time to get dinner started and maybe clean the downstairs bathroom and give the rugs a quick once-over before she got home.

She never said anything about it, but he figured he should do the major share of the housework, as long as she was working so hard at the newspaper. Besides, she never thought about dinner until she got home, and often she was too tired and cranky to figure out what to have, much less prepare it.

He decided on couscous with vegetables. Mo ate whatever she could grab during the day, and that most often meant deep fat fried, so Doug made an effort to cook healthy for them.

He was slicing the scallions when his office line rang.

"Douglas Stennett," he said, a bit breathless from the sprint from the kitchen. He really had to get a cordless.

"Hello, Douglas Stennett."

"Claudia. Hi."

"Is this a bad time?"

"No. This is fine. I was just getting started on dinner."

"You're eating so early? My God, you really have gone country."

"Actually, I'm preparing dinner."

"Excuse me? We must have a bad connection."

"Cute."

"As I remember, you had four specialties, five if you count cheeseburger as a separate dish from hamburger."

"Things change. I change." He slumped into his office swivel chair. Jack Roosevelt jumped heavily into his lap.

"Does that mean you even remembered Lawrence's birthday?"

"Of course. It's July 4."

"That's next week, lovey."

Doug reached for his desk calendar. "Oops," he said.

"Yeah, 'oops.' Are you planning to see him?"

"Yes. Absolutely. Maybe I could take him out for dinner."

"Good idea. His evenings don't get started until late these days, so you won't get in his way."

"Okay. We'll have dinner."

"We're going to my folks on the Fourth. Can you do it the night before?"

"Sure. That's fine. Does he still like computer games?"

"He'd play 24/7 if I let him."

"Maybe I could get him a computer game, then."

"Better not. I don't know what he's got already."

"Any other ideas?"

"Can you get Michael Jordan's autograph?"

"Probably not."

"He needs new socks and underwear."

"I don't want to get him socks and underwear."

"No. You want to get him something fun and be the hero, as always."

Doug saw Mo's car take the turn—too fast, as always—and slide to a stop at a 45-degree angle to the deck railing.

"I've got to go. Kiss them both for me."

"I'll kiss Cyndy. I'm lucky if Lawrence lets me in the same room with him these days. Doug?"

"Yeah?"

"He wears boxers."

"Thanks a lot."

"Say 'hi' to Monona for me."

"Sure. And you say 'hi' to…"

"Old what's-his-name. I will, lovey."

He met Mo in the entry hall. "Hi. I hoped to have dinner further along."

"What are we having?"

"Couscous."

"What else?"

"Uh, couscous with lots of stuff in it?"

"Couscous is a side dish, like rice or potatoes."

"Oh. I guess I should have known that, huh?"

"That's okay. We can get a pizza delivered. Were you on the phone?"

"Claudia."

"How's dear Claudia?" She followed him into the kitchen.

"One hundred percent Claudia. Would you care for a dry, unpretentious little white wine?"

"Could you serve it on the terrace?"

"You bet."

She had her shoes off and her feet up and was reading the morning paper when he brought her wine out to the screened porch. He sat on the bench next to her and popped open the beer he had brought for himself.

"What did Weilman say?" she asked.

"He wants me to recommend some investments for him. Computer software, too."

"A real client."

"Two in one week. I'm on a roll."

"That's right. What does Krueger want you to do?"

"He's interested in buying the diner. He wants me to make the inquiries. I guess I'll talk to the oldest brother. What's his name?"

"Rafe. Did you ask Weilman about Charlie for me?"

"Didn't have to. He dove in on his own. Says he was a grand guy but a lousy businessman. Oh, and he said he wants you to talk to him. Says he's got some stuff for you you'll be able to use."

They sat together, sipping and reading, until the pizza arrived, half pepperoni and sausage for her, half vegetarian for him, and they ate on the porch, watching the sun sink behind the poplars down by the pond.

"It really is heaven here," Mo murmured before shoving half a slice of pizza into her mouth.

"Worth giving up everything for?"

"I brought all the important stuff with me. What about you? Any regrets?"

"Not if I can figure out a way to earn a living here in the wilds."

"You've got a good start."

"I hope so."

Jack Roosevelt twined their legs, purring loudly.

"Did you get anything useful from that coach?" Doug asked after a long silence.

"Not really. Charlie was an upstanding citizen, a stand-up guy, pillar of the community. I'm hearing that a lot."

"What do you want, a scandal?"

"Of course not—although it would sell papers. He told

me I should talk to Sabra Farnum. She worked for Charlie at the diner."

"The tattooed lady?"

"And I thought you weren't meeting any of the locals."

"Just the ones with tattoos."

Mo finished her wine.

"You want a refill?"

"No, thanks. I'm going to work a little before bed."

"At least bring the laptop out here so you can enjoy the sunset."

"Good idea."

When she didn't get up right away, he looked a question at her.

"Something about talking with that coach today," she said slowly, running her finger around the rim of the wine glass. "Something not right."

"Bad vibes, huh?"

"Yes, Mr. Rational. Bad vibes. He was holding something back."

"Like what?"

"I don't know, but something." She put her wine glass behind her on the table. "Why did Claudia call?" she asked.

"She wanted to make sure I hadn't forgotten Lawrence's birthday."

"Isn't it on the Fourth?"

"Yeah. But I forgot that July comes right after June this year. I'm going to take him out to dinner."

"In Chicago?"

"Yeah. She's taking them to see her folks in Winnetka for the Fourth, so I'll take him out the night before."

"You'll miss the parade."

"No, I won't. I'll drive back the same night."

"That's silly. You'd be exhausted."

"I'd be fine."

"Whatever." Mo shoved to her feet.

"Hold on. Don't 'whatever' me."

"I want you to see your son, Douglas."

"I know you do. You've been very understanding."

"Oh, please."

He got up quickly, taking her hands in his. "You have. You've been wonderful about the whole situation."

"They're good kids, Doug. You and Claudia did a good job with them."

"They're practically grown-up."

"They still need you, Doug. They need to know you're in their lives and that you love them."

"I know." He squeezed her hands. "You're amazing," he said.

"That's me."

They held hands a moment more. The peep frogs had started up down by the pond.

"Do you have a lot of work to do?"

"Always, but I'm not going to do a lot tonight."

"Good. I'll miss you."

They kissed lightly and went to their offices.

"You ought to be talking to Sabra. Sabra thought the world of Charlie."

Sylvia Farnum sat in a swivel chair behind the counter in the waiting area of the Hair Apparent Beauty Salon, her legs dangling over the footrest. Mo sat in the other swivel chair.

"I will," Mo said. "In fact, I was hoping you could tell me where she is. Nobody answers the phone at her house."

"She's like that. Hates phones. She'll be showing up at the diner pretty soon, though. She and the other angels are building a float for the parade."

"A float?"

"Kind of a tribute to Charlie. Lord, but Sabes loved that man. They all did. 'Charlie's Angels,' they called themselves."

Sylvia twirled a strand of her raven hair around her index finger. A cobra tattoo coiled up the right side of her neck to just under the ear. Her twin, Sabra's, snake went up the left side. That's how Mo had learned to tell them apart, that and the fact that Sabra smoked 'tobacco cigarettes,' as

Sylvia called them. Sylvia limited herself to the occasional cigar.

"Did Charlie ever date any of the angels?"

Sylvia whooped and put her hand to her breast. "Charlie! Good Lord, no!"

"Why is that funny?"

Her long, slender fingers—made still longer by three-inch false nails—fluttered back to her hair. "I just never thought of Charlie that way, I guess," she said.

"He didn't have a lady friend in Madison?"

"Not that I'd know of. Not that I'd know. Like I said, you ought to be talking to Sabra."

"So, tell me about the float."

"It's supposed to look like the diner."

"Great idea."

"Stupid idea. I got a better idea. If they want to pay tribute to Charlie, somebody ought to catch the son of a bitch who killed him and string him up on the highest tree in Fireman's Park. Now, that would be a tribute." She hopped to her feet and started lining up her tools on the shelf by the sink.

"You think somebody murdered Charlie?"

Sylvia snorted. "I sure as hell do," she said.

"Why?"

She tapped a long-toothed comb against her teeth. "I always had this feeling with Charlie," she said. "Even when he was joking around. It made me think something bad was going to happen to him. And now it has." She shook her head. "Does that sound completely nuts?"

"Not really. I hadn't thought of it in those words, but I felt it, too."

"Poor Charlie," Sylvia said.

"Poor Charlie," Mo agreed.

"Hey! There she goes!"

"There who goes?" Mo turned to look out the window and saw Sabra Farnum walking from her car parked on Main around to the back of the diner.

"Go talk to Sabra," Sylvia said again. "She thought the world of Charlie."

"So, whattaya think?" Sabra asked when she saw Mo walking across the dirt field behind the diner. "Do you think it looks like Charlie's?"

Sabra held a dripping paintbrush and had a cigarette dangling from her mouth. Mo appraised the plywood lump Sabra had just started painting.

"If you say so," Mo said.

"You're right. It looks like shit."

"I didn't say that!"

"Wait'll we get the roof on. You'll at least be able to tell it's supposed to be a building."

Mo walked slowly around the ramshackle model, which squatted about six feet long by four feet wide by six feet high without the roof.

"How, exactly, were you planning on making it move?"

Sabra took a long drag on her cigarette without touching it with her hand. "How's that?" she asked, expelling a cloud of smoke.

"It's for a parade, right?"

Sabra looked from Mo back to the float. "I see your point," she said. "We'll have to get some wheels under the son of a bitch."

"Wheels would be good."

Sabra perched the paintbrush on the edge of the roofless mini-diner, spit her cigarette into the dirt to the side, and picked up the pack from the ground to get a fresh smoke.

"Your sister thinks somebody killed Charlie," Mo said.

"I think Syl reads too many bad novels. This isn't New York City. You know what I'm saying?"

"Sure."

"Then again, it only takes one, doesn't it?'

"That's true. Did anybody have it in for Charlie?"

"Just that foundling Charlie took in. Pete something or other. Charlie had to can him a couple of weeks back."

"Why? It would take a lot to make Charlie fire somebody."

"Ain't I the living proof of that?" Sabra laughed. "Caught him stealing food. That's one thing Charlie could not abide, was a thief. Other than that, he seemed like a pretty good kid."

"How long did this Pete work for Charlie?"

Sabra shrugged. "Six months, maybe. He was here through the winter. I kept thinking when the weather warmed up, he'd take off that stupid stocking cap of his, and we'd get to see what the top of his head looked like."

Mo looked over at the back door of the diner, which was still sealed with the yellow crime scene tape. "Okay if I take a look around?" she asked.

"You're free, white, and 21. Just don't let that cute little deputy catch you."

Mo walked over to the large dumpster by the door. White letters on the sides warned "DO NOT PLAY ON DUMPSTER."

"When does that get collected?" Mo asked.

"Tuesdays and Fridays, usually. I don't think they've been by since Charlie got killed, though."

"Do you keep it locked?"

"Nope. We don't gift wrap the garbage, either. What exactly are you looking for?"

"No idea." Mo reached up and shoved on the lid, which

gave a reluctant inch. She strained, trying to get enough muscle under the lid to throw it back on its hinges.

"Let me help, Hon."

"If you could just hold it open." She threw a leg over the top and rolled, tumbling to the bottom with a hollow banging.

"Are you all right?!" she heard Sabra call from outside.

"Define 'all right.'"

Even though the dumpster was nearly empty, it bore the scent of garbage past, and slime coated the bottom. Mo found nothing that might even resemble a clue.

Getting out was tougher than getting in. When Sabra leaned in to give Mo a hand up, the lid cracked the back of Mo's head.

"Damn! I am so sorry," Sabra said when Mo was finally back on solid ground. "I didn't mean to skull you like that. You okay?"

"No worse than when I started, I guess."

"Tell me something, then. Just why did you want to go mucking around in that sty?"

"I read too many Nancy Drew books when I was a kid, I guess."

Sabra laughed and took a last drag on her cigarette. "So, you think maybe this Pete character murdered Charlie?"

"We seem to be short on suspects otherwise."

"I suppose. But I don't think Pete killed Charlie or anybody else."

"Why's that?"

"The little shit was no killer. A space cadet, yeah, but not nasty."

"Wouldn't hurt a fly, huh?"

"As a matter of fact, I saw him trap a fly in a cup and let it out the back door more than once."

"But the fly didn't fire him for stealing."

"True."

"Where's Pete now?"

"Hanged if I know. He hasn't been around since Charlie canned him."

"Do you know where he lives?"

"In a trailer out by the old county dump. He biked all the way in, even in a blizzard."

"Could you tell me how to find it?"

"I can tell you how to find the dump." Sabra pointed south along the county road that bisected the highway and proceeded to give directions that included "Turn left at the mailbox that's shaped like a tractor" and "Go three roads past the old Hollister place."

"I'd better write that down," Mo said.

"You thinking of going out there now?"

Mo shrugged. "I could help you paint a little bit first, if you've got an extra brush."

Sabra smiled. "I got plenty of brushes," she said, and together they walked back to Charlie's float.

· · · ·

"Thanks for seeing me," Doug said.

"No problem. I got 20 minutes before my next class."

Rafe Connell walked ahead of Doug into a huge room filled with machinery. Not knowing a lathe from a drill press, Doug could only guess at its functions.

Rafe went to the front of the room and plopped onto a stool in front of the biggest chalkboard Doug had ever seen. Not finding a chair or a second stool, Doug stood, feeling foolish and wishing he hadn't brought his attaché case.

Rafe lit a cigarette, shook the match out, flicked it on the floor. "What can I do for you?" he asked.

"I may have a buyer for the diner, if you're interested in selling."

Rafe picked at a scab on his elbow. "I'd sell the place in a minute," he said, "if I owned it." He took a long drag on the cigarette. "Mom owns the dump," he said. "I don't know if she wants to sell it. You'd have to ask her."

"Charlie left the diner to your mother?"

Rafe snorted. "Charlie didn't own it. Mom did. She pretty much owned Charlie, too." Rafe picked a strand of tobacco from his teeth. "Charlie was always a mama's boy." He looked past Doug. "Logan! How nice of you to put in an appearance."

Doug turned to see a thin young man take his place at one of the workstations three quarters of the way back in the room.

"I've been sick," he said. "Did I miss anything?"

"No, Logan. You didn't miss a thing. I just come here every day so they'll pay me at the end of the month."

"They pay you for this?"

"You're a riot, Logan. You need help on your project?"

"Yeah. I got a couple questions."

Rafe shot an inquiring look at Doug. "We about done here?" he asked, sliding off the stool and starting toward the back of the room.

"One more thing," Doug said. "Does your mom own the diner free and clear?"

"Damned if I know. No, wait a minute. I do know. Charlie talked her into taking a good chunk of cash out of it about six months ago. I think the bank's got the note. I only know because she called me to ask if I'd countersign."

"Did you?"

"Hell no."

"Who did?"

"No idea."

"Why did Charlie need the money?"

"Don't know that either. And I guess old Charlie isn't in any shape to tell you."

"No," Doug agreed. "He sure isn't."

With that, Rafe turned his attention to his student, and the interview was over.

He was always nervous when he had to meet a stranger, and having to confront Charlene Connell was an agony.

Still, this interview was the next step in establishing his consulting business. He couldn't just sit at his computer and crunch stats on baseball trades while Mo supported them both.

He parked the CR-V in front of a small one-story frame house a block north of Main Street and two blocks south of Fireman's Park. How would he start the conversation? What if she didn't want to talk at all? Would she start crying?

Okay, he thought grimly, walking up the narrow walk. You're scared. Now do it anyway.

But he needn't have worried about getting Mama Connell to talk. She wanted, needed to talk about her dead son.

"Charlie did all the cooking," she told him after getting him settled in a comfortable armchair and serving him a glass of iced tea. "Omelets were his specialty, of course, but he could cook anything. He made wonderful stirfries. Never used a recipe. He was like a fella who plays the piano without needing any music. Little pinch of this, a shake of that. He just had the touch."

"Mo tells me you baked all the pies."

She nodded, smiling. "Charlie said nobody made pies like his mama."

Framed photos of Charlie and his brothers in various stair-step poses covered most of the flat surfaces, including the piano keyboard. White lace doilies decorated the matching armchairs. An ancient copper colored cocker spaniel, muzzle white, eyes droopy and runny, curled at Charlene Connell's feet. A plastic magazine rack held well-thumbed mail order catalogs.

But the Norman Rockwell still life had some modern touches. Doug spotted Coldwater Creek, not Sears, atop the catalogs, and a cordless phone sat atop the neat fan of magazines—*Good Housekeeping, Midwest Living, The National Enquirer*, was that really *Barron's*?—on the coffee table.

As if prompted by his glance, the phone chirped. Charlene Connell scooped it up instantly.

"'Lo. Hi, there, Alice. How are you, dear? Uh huh. Uh huh." She covered the mouthpiece with her small, pudgy hand. "Alice Featherston. She's a talker!" And then "Uh huh" into the phone, and, "Oh, dear! How awful! I don't know how you endure it. Listen, Alice... Alice? Alice, dear. I've got company. Yes. No, no. That's all right, dear. I'll call you back in a bit. Okay, dear. You, too. Bye now."

"There, now," Charlene Connell said, putting the phone back on the magazine cradle. "Where were we?"

Punctuated by three more phone calls in 20 minutes, Charlene took Doug through Charlie's childhood. He was the baby of the family, third of three boys, left fatherless while still in diapers. Rumor had it the father had run off to California with another woman, but nobody knew for sure. Charlie was a quiet boy, who preferred hanging around the kitchen helping his Mama to playing football or fooling around with cars with his older brothers—and an indifferent scholar who worked hard to get C's. The wrestling team was the only thing he tried for.

"And sometimes," Charlene admitted, "Charlie would just sit. My Charlie was a dreamer."

"What did he dream about, Mrs. Connell?"

"You call me Charlene, dear. From the time he was tiny, he wanted to run the diner. Betsy and Russ Cramer had it then, and they let Charlie sit on a stool in back of the counter and watch Betsy work the grill and Russ get the Cokes and phosphates and make the sodas—it was more of an ice cream parlor back then. I'm not sure when he stopped watching and started helping out, but he was working the counter by the time he could see over it."

Charlene shook her head, smiling at the memory. "Other boys want to be cowboys or athletes and that. But my Charlie wanted to run the diner. And that's just what he did."

"He took over the diner before he got out of high school?"

"He sure did. Russ had the arthritis bad, and he and Betsy really wanted to get out from under. By that time, there wasn't anyone they'd rather sell to than Charlie, the diner being like a second home to him. He'd been saving every nickel he made from Russ and Betsy and what he made from the paper route and odd jobs, shoveling snow in the winter and yard work in the summer. That boy worked all the time when he wasn't with the wrestling team. I was able to help him when he was short on the down payment, because I had a little inheritance from my daddy. Charlie kept up with the monthlies and paid off every nickel of what I loaned him. He did without, my Charlie. Took nothing out of the business for himself."

Charlene pulled a white embroidered hankie from the sleeve of her house dress and dabbed at her eyes.

"But you kept the title in your name?"

"Yes."

"Why was that?"

"Charlie never had any interest in the business end of things. I took care of all that. He said he'd feel better if I were listed as the owner."

"I understand," Doug said, watching the woman's eyes, "that Charlie had recently taken out a loan against the diner. Would you have any idea why he might have needed a large amount of money?"

Doug watched helplessly as Charlene's composure dissolved in a flashflood of tears. No lace hankie could possibly staunch this flow. But the ancient cocker knew what to do. He roused with a groan and put his head on Charlene's leg.

"Sweet old Topsy," she murmured. "You're just a precious. That's what you are." She stroked the old dog absently while the weeping ran its course.

"I'll get us more tea," she said abruptly, rising and taking up Doug's glass.

Doug heard the opening and closing of the refrigerator, the tinkling of ice cubes in glasses, the pouring of tea from pitcher into glass.

"He did it for me," she said when she returned. Her face was tear-streaked and pale. "He wanted to build a new house for us out by the lake. He'd talked about it for years. He bought the land as soon as he paid off the diner. He said it would be our house, but I knew he'd go on living in that horrid little basement."

Her chest heaved. She put the saturated hankie to her mouth, sniffled, and sighed.

"He could have swung it without the loan," she continued. "But any way I ran the numbers, the tax deduction on the equity loan more than made up for the interest on the loan. That's about the only deduction a small business person has left, you know."

Doug's surprise must have shown. Charlene smiled. "Like I said, I handled all the finances," she said.

The phone rang again, giving Doug a chance to digest this new information. He had an answer for Mo as to why Charlie had borrowed $30,000. But he still didn't know what had happened to it.

"Rose McGreevey," Charlene said when she had snapped off the phone. "Wants to know if I'll be at the book group tonight. We're discussing *Angela's Ashes*. Have you read it?"

"No. I think Mo did."

"It's so depressing." She laughed. "They're all trying to keep me busy," she said, nodding toward the phone. "It's very dear of them. Raphael has been calling almost every day. He used to call once a week, Sunday morning, right before I went to church. He knew I'd only be able to talk for a few minutes."

"Raphael is an unusual name," Doug said.

"Everybody calls him Rafe. Athanasius is the middle son. He's 10 months younger."

"I suppose those names got them into a few fistfights in school," Doug offered.

"Do you think so? If we'd had a girl, I was going to name her Talitha."

"The little girl Jesus raised from the dead."

"That's right!" Her eyes smiled over the rim of her iced tea.

Doug grinned. "I pick up some of that from Mo."

"You're wondering where 'Charlie' came from, right?"

He hadn't been, but he nodded.

"I named the first two. My husband said two was enough. He finally agreed to a third, only on the condition that he get to name it. He called him Charlie for me, the dear man. He would have named a girl Charlene.

"I'm awfully glad we had Charlie," she added. "Oh, the others are fine boys. But Charlie, he was my special baby. Right from the first."

Doug took a sip of the sweet tea. "What's the secret of your famous pies?" he asked.

"Oh, child. It's no secret. You use all fresh, and you don't beat up the crust. The less you handle it, the better. That and scoops of sugar and tubs of real butter."

"What's your best pie?"

"Charlie just adored my lemon meringue. Personally, I favor the Dutch apple. Cherry, raspberry, strawberry. Chocolate peanut butter. Banana cream. Folks seem to love them all." She fumbled for the hankie. "I guess I won't be baking all those pies any more."

"Actually, that's what I came to talk to you about, Mrs. Connell."

"Charlene, dear."

"Right. I have a client who's interested in buying the diner."

"Andy Krueger," she said immediately.

"Why, yes."

"He kept after Charlie for years to sell him the diner. He wants to turn it into a lawn and garden store."

"Not a diner?"

"Heavens, no. What does he know about diners?"

"Couldn't he just build an addition to his hardware store?"

"He wants my building."

Doug shook his head. "Help me here."

"The diner has a huge extra basement. Charlie never

used it for anything. Andy wants it for storage. He thinks it would be a lot cheaper than building from scratch."

"But you don't want to sell it to him?"

"Oh, no!" She put a fist to her breast. "I'm hoping someone will want to keep the diner going. It can be a real money maker."

"How much would Charlie take in on a Saturday? If you don't mind my asking."

"I don't mind at all, dear. But I have to tell you, the reason they didn't find any money was because Charlie took it to the bank Saturday afternoon. He didn't want to have large amounts of money sitting over Sunday. Clive Baxter always opened up special for him Saturday afternoon."

She set her iced tea on a coaster, sat back, and folded her hands in her lap.

"I feel bad having to ask about this, but what about the money from the mortgage he took out on the diner?"

Charlene shook her head. "Charlie never touched it," she said, her voice cracking. "Clive just kept it at the bank to pay for the property.

"No," she said decisively. "It wasn't for money. Somebody killed my baby, but it wasn't for money. It was somebody Charlie knew. I just know it."

"What makes you say that?"

"My Charlie knew how to take care of himself. Folks thought he was soft, because he talked so quiet. But Charlie was strong. He'd been through a lot. And he was careful. Folks thought he was crazy, taking in strays and putting them to work the way he did. But Charlie was always in control. Whoever did that to him…" She took a shuddering breath. "It was somebody he knew. Somebody he trusted."

Doug just nodded.

"I don't believe in an eye for an eye," she said. "Jesus

brought us a better teaching. I just can't stand the thought of whoever did this walking around free. It isn't right."

The old cocker again plopped his head on Charlene Connell's leg for stroking.

"I understand," Doug said, standing up.

"I know you do, dear," Charlene said.

"And I'm so sorry about your son."

"I know." She reached up and patted Doug's cheek gently. "It shows."

From the refuge of his car, Doug looked back at the little home. What manner of woman, he wondered, had been able to raise three sons by herself, in a tiny little house, and take care of one son's finances in the bargain.

A very strong one, he decided.

Better tell Mo we can rule out robbery as a motive, he thought as he pulled away. He caught himself and smiled. Looks like one of the Hardy Boys married Nancy Drew, he thought.

. . . .

"You didn't ask me what I seen the night Charlie was murdered."

Mo's heart gave a quick skip. She had finished interviewing Dan Weilman for what she was still telling everyone was a story about Charlie for the *Doings* but which, she realized, had become something much more to her.

"The Sheriff says it was an accident," she said.

"The Sheriff's a stupid asshole. Excuse me. I'd bet cash money Charlie was murdered. And I might just have seen the guy who did it."

Mo waited, fighting the impulse to press. She leaned against the video store counter. Dan was at his post in the director's chair on the other side.

"I'm open to 10 on Saturdays, okay? So, I'm sitting right

here Saturday night, just like I am now, looking out the window, and here comes Charlie, walking in the pouring rain. I figure he's been to the Fireman's parade committee meeting. If there was a committee, Charlie was on it and probably running it.

"I also figure he stopped off for a couple of toots at the VFW and that maybe that's a six-pack he's carrying. Charlie liked his beer all right.

"Anyway, it's raining like a bastard, which is maybe why I don't see right away that there's somebody with Charlie. The other guy starts waving his hands, like Charlie's trying to sell him something the guy is definitely not buying."

"Did you recognize this other person?"

"Naw. I just saw him from the back."

"Then what happened?"

"I'm thinking Charlie's getting a real bellyful of this guy and might just pop him one. And here I am with the best seat in the house for the Saturday night fights. Charlie had a temper on him. He'd fool you, talking so soft and all, but I seen him go off more than once. But Charlie just walks around to the side door, and leaves the other fellow standing there."

"What did this other fellow do?"

"Walked off. But see, I figure he might have come back later, still good and sore."

"What did he look like? That you could see."

"It was really raining, like I said. And Charlie don't keep a light on in front. Didn't. The guy was wearing a stocking cap. I remember that, because it struck me as strange."

"You're sure it was a man?"

Dan considered that. "That's interesting you'd say that. I guess it could have been a female. He, or she, was pretty short. Almost as short as me."

"But you didn't see any actual fighting?"

"No. But like I say, the guy could have come back later. They were having one hell of an argument."

"Hmmm. Well, thank you so much," Mo said as she tucked her pencil into the spiral of her notebook. "You've been very helpful. Oh, and I understand you and my husband are doing a little business."

"He's a smart man."

"Yes, he is."

"A tad on the conservative side, though. Financially, anyway."

Mo hesitated. "There's one thing that bothers me about what you told me," she said.

"Yeah? What's that?"

"You said you were sitting down, like you are now, when you saw Charlie having the argument in front of the diner, right?"

"Yeah. I was right here, like always."

"But from where you're sitting, you can't see over the counter, can you?"

Surprise registered on Dan's face. He gnawed at his knuckle. "I guess I must have been standing up," he said.

"I guess you must have been," Mo agreed, smiling pleasantly as she flipped her notebook shut and left.

This wasn't exactly what she'd had in mind when she took the job, Mo reflected as she sat on the floor, surrounded by bundles of newspapers, frantically sorting by zip code to get them to the post office before it closed.

She knew that editing a weekly wasn't going to be glamorous. She knew her work days would stretch beyond all reason. But this week, with Jeanne Appleton gone to Badger State Forensics in Madison, Vi out sick, and Bruce nowhere to be seen, it came down to Mo and the newspapers and 47 minutes to get them bundled and to the post office.

She might just make it if she didn't get interrupted.

"Hey, Mokwin."

"Hey, Dilly."

"You busy?"

"Pretty much, yeah."

"Whatcha doing?"

"Shooting ducks in a rain barrel."

"No, you're not. You're sorting the papers."

"Yep. And I'm in a big hurry."

"I'll help you."

"Oh, Dill. I don't know. That's really nice…"

"I can do it. Just show me."

What the hey, she thought. I might as well have company while I go crazy.

"Okay. Come here."

Dilly skipped in happily and flopped down next to her.

"See this number on the label?"

He nodded.

"We need to put all the numbers that match together. All five numbers have to be the same. See?"

Dilly kept nodding. He picked up one of the unsorted papers, frowned at it, and then grinned at her, as if he had caught her trying to trick him.

"Let me see something," he said.

He scooted from pile to pile, checking the labels. He put the paper he was holding onto one of the piles, grinned, and picked up another paper. He flipped it onto another pile.

Mo resumed her sorting, falling into the mindless rhythm that let her pick, scan, and pitch papers without pausing. The tightly rolled papers in their brown wrappers thudded softly.

"The first two numbers are always the same," Dilly said after awhile.

"For all the ones in southern Wisconsin. You'll get some for other places."

"What other places?"

"Florida. California. Miles City, Montana."

"This is fun."

Mo laughed. "If you say so."

After a few minutes, he was sorting faster than she was, barely glancing at the labels before flinging the papers. Could he possibly be doing them right, she wondered. He was grinning, his tongue sticking out at the corner of his mouth.

"I'm going to get the sacks and start bagging them," she said.

"Okay," Dilly said happily, without pausing.

She brought the cloth sacks from the back room, shook one open, and began scooping papers into the bag. She glanced at the labels, pretending to be straightening them to get them to fit snugly.

"Did I make any mistakes?"

"Not so far."

His huge smile made her smile back. "I'm good at this," he said.

"You're very good at this."

The jangling phone made her jump. "*Doings.* This is Mo."

"Hello?" A female voice, young and afraid.

"Yes? May I help you?"

Silence.

"Who is this?"

"I go to the high school with Marcus."

Mo frowned. Marcus? Ah, the wrestler and student body vice president.

"Go ahead."

"I'm Cindy."

Another long pause.

"Cindy? I'm in a bit of a rush here. Could I call you back?"

"No. I'll call you." The connection broke.

"I'm all done!" Dilly announced.

"You are amazing."

Dilly helped her carry the bags the block and a half down Main to the post office. They made it with four minutes to spare.

"I really couldn't have done it without you," she told him.

"You're welcome, Mokwin. You know what? The bakery is open."

"Is it now? It's awfully late."

"They're baking in back. I smelled it."

"That's right. Julia bakes cookies for her mail orders on Wednesdays."

"I like peanut butter chocolate chip the best."

"That's my favorite, too."

"They cost 35 cents."

"How about I treat?"

"O-kay!"

Julia van Dender's peanut butter chocolate chip cookies, fresh from the oven, were lightly crisped on the outside, warm and moist on the inside, and all good. Mo and Dilly sat out on the curb, legs in the street, eating them. Dilly smacked his lips when he chewed.

She smoothed her copy of the *Doings* out on her lap and read:

> CHARLIE CONNELL DEAD AT AGE 43:
> "LOOKS LIKE AN ACCIDENT"—SHERIFF
>
> Charlie Connell, 43, was found dead in the basement of Charlie's Mitchell Diner, a business he owned at 147 Main Street, at around 4:30 Sunday morning, according to Dane County Sheriff Roger Repoz.
>
> "He apparently died from injuries sustained from a fall down the basement steps," Repoz said. Connell's mother, Charlene Connell, found him after he failed to answer her telephone call around 4:00 a.m., Repoz added.

"Mokwin? I'm done with my cookie."

"You want to take a little walk?"

Dilly nodded.

They walked down Main, past the diner, which would have been closed this late in the afternoon anyway but which now felt abandoned to Mo.

"I go in there," Dilly said.

"Into the diner?"

"Yeah."

"How come?"

"It makes me feel not so sad. Are you going to tell?"

"Of course not."

They walked down to the river, the mud sucking at their shoes.

"I miss Charlie," Dilly said. "It hurts my heart."

"It hurts my heart, too."

"He was my friend."

"And you were a good friend to him."

"He's dead."

"Yes."

"I know what happens when you die. Your body goes into the ground, but your soul goes to heaven to be with Jesus."

"That sounds right to me."

"I'll see Charlie when I die."

"Don't be in any rush, though. I need you here."

"Okay."

"We'd better head back."

"Okay. Mokwin? Can I sort papers with you next day?"

"I only sort the papers once a week, on Wednesdays."

His face darkened.

"But I can use a good man like you around the office for other things, too," she said.

"O-kay!" Dilly said, turning to start walking back to town.

. . . .

Doug spent most of the day doing everything but the thing he most needed to do.

He finished his report for Dan Weilman, recommending a balanced portfolio of relatively low-risk investments designed to pay off for the patient, long-term investor. Then he puttered on line with his favorite business news sources for over an hour. He baked cranberry muffins. He dusted the blinds in the living room and his office. He changed the sheets and started a load of wash. He pulled weeds in the garden, letting Jack Roosevelt sun himself.

And then, not feeling any more ready than when he began procrastinating, he went inside and called Andy Krueger.

"I've been waiting to hear from you!" Andy said when Doug identified himself. "Hold on a minute."

Doug heard Andy's muffled voice and another voice.

"Sorry. I'm working the counter."

"If this is a bad time…"

"No, no. This is fine. What did you find out? Will they sell?"

"Actually, Mrs. Connell owns the diner."

"Yeah? How much does she want for it?"

"She not ready to sell."

"How's that? Hold on. All the way back, past garden hoses. Unless we sold them already. You still there?"

"Yeah."

"It's a madhouse around here. I got Elmer and Walt out sick. Why don't she want to sell?"

"She wants to make sure it stays a diner. She seems to think you have other plans for it."

"Where'd she get an idea like that?"

"She says you were after Charlie to sell it so you could turn it into a lawn and garden center."

"Is that a fact? What do you figure the place is worth?"

"Don't know. I could check it out."

"You do that. Then we'll make Mama an offer too good to turn down. You know, I'm starting to like having my own personal business manager. Listen, I gotta run. I'm up to my armpits here. You get back to me, okay now?"

The line went dead. Scowling, Doug recradled the phone. Andy Krueger hadn't seemed at all surprised that Charlene Connell didn't want to sell the diner, and he didn't deny having plans to convert the diner to other uses.

That didn't make him a murderer, by any means, Doug reflected when he realized where his thoughts were drifting. But it did make him a liar.

She could hear Doug whistling over the whirring of the mixer. The man did everything with enthusiasm. The thought made her smile.

She had her feet up, pumps off, luxuriating in the rare chance to work the Sunday *New York Times* crossword, which she kept around all week, just in case.

He appeared at the kitchen door, a grin on his face, an apron strapped to his waist. "Tuna puff surprise now being served," he announced.

"Great." She lifted Jack Roosevelt gently off her lap.

Mo didn't really like tuna puff surprise—or any kind of food with the word "surprise" in it—but she was grateful that Doug had taken charge of the evening meal.

"How's the mystery coming?" Doug asked after she had properly praised the taste and presentation of the meal.

"I know you think I'm a little over the top on this," she said, picking a cucumber from her salad. "But I'm more convinced than ever that Charlie was murdered."

"Why's that?"

She told Doug what Dan Weilman had told her about

the man in the stocking cap he saw arguing with Charlie outside the diner the night Charlie died.

"And you think that he might be this Pete, the dishwasher Sabra told you about?"

"Could be. But Sabra says Pete literally wouldn't hurt a fly." She speared a cherry tomato and forked it into her mouth. "I'm thinking this Pete sounds like the kid who rescued Cora Beth Watkins' dog, and that hardly sounds like a killer. Besides, there's no real motive."

"I might be able to help you there."

She looked up. "The loan?"

"No. Charlene Connell explained that. She said Charlie used the money to buy land to build her a house. She says he never even laid his hands on any actual money."

"What, then?"

"Andy Krueger wants to turn the diner into a lawn and garden store."

"So?"

"So Krueger approaches Charlie about selling. Charlie turns him down. Krueger goes ballistic."

"And kills Charlie over a building?"

"It could happen."

"I don't think so."

Doug sagged. "I guess I'm no great sleuth, huh?" he said. "And no great cook, either."

He had already finished his puff and salad and was working on his second bread stick.

"No! It's delicious." She popped a large bite of puff into her mouth.

"I did some checking into Krueger's finances," he said while she ate. "He's overextended."

"Some checking, you say?"

"Well, yeah. That information isn't hard to get."

"If I had gotten it, you would have called it 'meddling.'"

He waved a half-eaten bread stick at her. "Just trying to be helpful," he said.

"And I thank you. I really do."

They did the dishes together and settled in on the living room sofa, she with her stack of proofs, he with his *Wall Street Journal.* After a few minutes, Doug leaned over and nibbled her right ear.

"My goodness. You fix me dinner. You do some meddling for me. And now you're offering to be my love slave?"

The home phones exploded, the outlet in Doug's office bleating first, the kitchen phone jangling a half-beat later.

"Let it ring," Doug said.

"Better not."

"I'll get it."

"Thanks."

He loped into the den. Jack Roosevelt hopped onto the couch and curled up in the spot where Doug had been sitting.

"It's for you," Doug said, emerging from the office. "Pierpont."

"Really?"

"Do we know anybody else who sounds like a garbage disposal grinding glass?"

"Nope. He's the only one. But he's never called at home before."

"First time for everything. Maybe he wants to offer you a huge raise."

"Right." She went into the kitchen and picked up the phone. "Hello?"

"Horace Adamski says we ought to leave dead dogs lie."

"He didn't say anything like that to me."

"He says Charlie Connell's death was accidental. He says you should write up a good story and quit snooping around."

"And you're telling me not to report the story of his death?"

She saw Doug scowling from the doorway.

"Last time I looked at the masthead, it said I'm the publisher and you're the editor. Where I come from, that means I get to tell you what to do."

"Yeah. It's the same where I come from." She fought to keep her voice level against the anger swirling up in her.

"Glad to hear that's the way they do it in the big city, too."

"Mr. Pierpont, in the big city, reporters get paid for snooping around."

"That's fine. Dig up all the dirt you can on those imbeciles on the school board. That ought to keep you busy."

"But not on the possible murder of one of Mitchell's most prominent citizens?"

"If it's an accident, and we say something different, we look like idiots."

"What do we look like if the *Cardinal-Herald* breaks the story, our story, before we do?"

"You aren't in the big city now. When Millie's Aunt Maudie from Des Moines pays her a visit, we're on the story like flies on stink. We got the exclusive pictures when Elmer Vasco grows a zucchini shaped like Richard Nixon's head. But we don't run rumors and speculation about murders that never happened."

"Do we run news stories about murders that did?"

"Maybe you'd better take another look at that masthead."

"That sounds like a threat."

"Don't be melodramatic. That kind of stuff only happens in the big city."

"What happens in the small town?"

"Life, as they say, goes on."

She took a deep breath. "We need to talk about this."

"I thought that's what we're doing."

"I mean face-to-face."

"Come on in any time you like."

The click of the phone left an unnatural silence behind. Doug took the phone from her and recradled it.

Mo shook her head. "Adamski's putting pressure on Pierpont not to run anything on Charlie's death," she said. "Maybe the biggest story this town's seen in decades."

"So what now? Time to dust off the resume?"

"No way!"

"Somehow, I knew you'd say that."

"I think I need to talk with Morgan Winslow."

"Who?"

"My immediate predecessor at the *Doings*. I've heard that his leaving was on less than friendly terms. But first, I have an appointment to interview Mitchell's very own diva."

Nikki von Thoreaux was a one-woman show, on or off the stage. Now she was performing for Mo.

"You heard a clanging?" Mo prompted.

"Not a clanging, exactly," Madam T decided, grabbing the tip of her nose with thumb and forefinger and giving it a vigorous squeeze and shake. "A loud thud. A metallic thud. But a hollow sound. A door slamming, almost. Almost like a metal door slamming."

"And this was what time?"

Madam T waved the word away as if shooing a wasp. "The western concept of time really has no meaning," she said. "Transcending time allows one to enter into the creative vortex, becoming timeless, limitless."

They sat on the stage of the empty theater, daylight barely penetrating the thick black curtains drawn over all the windows. Even so, Madam T wore dark glasses, with sweeps of silver leaping from the tips, somehow suggesting to Mo both the wings of Mercury and the fins on a 1957 Chevy Bel Aire.

Madam T sat with her legs sticking out in front of her

on the floor. She wore an ankle-length black dress. Her straight, forest fire red hair flowed over her shoulders nearly to her waist.

"But it was Saturday night? The night Charlie died?"

"Late that night. Early the next morning." She shrugged. "It really doesn't matter." She took a long pull on her cigarette and leaned back, letting the smoke dribble over the edges of her mouth. Watching her made Mo want to take up smoking again.

"Yes," she said, aiming the dark lenses of her glasses at Mo. "It was the night Charlie died. I couldn't sleep, of course. I'm always flying after a performance. I was sitting right here, letting my energy merge with the energy left behind by the audience. This horrid noise shattered my karma, I can assure you."

"I'm sure it did."

Madam T arrived in Mitchell about a year before Mo became editor of the *Doings* and immediately set about renovating the old movie house, which had stood vacant for years on the side street that dead-ended at the river a block off Main. After six months, she opened her coffee house, introducing espresso to Mitchell. Another six months after that, she put posters in the frames on either side of the old ticket booth out front announcing the opening of "El Mondo Theatre," which occupied the upstairs of the old building.

She lived in the theater dressing room, an arrangement that struck local folks as abnormal at the least and probably downright immoral. And she lived with another woman.

Madam T served as producer, director, writer, and entire cast of the first performance at the El Mondo, "A Woman's Place." Mo attended opening night and watched Madam T become, among others, Susan B. Anthony, Bess Truman, Katherine Hepburn, Babe Didrikson Zaharias and, in an especially memorable scene, both Anita Hill and Clarence Thomas.

Just before intermission, Madam T as Emily Dickinson was singing, "Because I could not stop for death, he kindly stopped for me" to the tune of "The Yellow Rose of Texas" when she dropped to the stage and lay still for almost a minute.

Mo later learned that she had experienced a petite mal seizure. She had liked the effect so much, she incorporated the swoon into subsequent performances.

And there had been subsequent performances, despite Mitchell's almost total indifference to the presentation, for small groups of curiosity seekers from Madison and lovers of the avant garde and incomprehensible.

And now Madam T, with elaborate flourishes and a roller coaster of vocal inflections, was relating what might be an important clue to what might be the murder of Charlie Connell.

"So, you think it might have been a door slamming?" Mo pressed again.

"Noooooooooo." The sound seeped from her mouth the way the smoke had. "Not a car door, anyway." Madam T took another luxuriant drag on her cigarette. More snakes of smoke coiled her head.

Mo heard a movement and turned to see a short, stocky woman with short, blonde hair moving toward them.

"Hello, love. Didn't realize you had company."

"Gretch!" Madam T clapped her hands. "Come meet our lovely Ms. Monona Quinn."

"Howdy!" Gretch bent down, and Madam T turned her head and tilted it to receive a lip brush on the cheek. Gretch wore tattered denim cut offs and a frayed gray sweatshirt with a large, truculent Bucky Badger, the mascot of the university in Madison, striding across her breasts.

"Meet the other half of the El Mondo creative team," Madam T announced.

"Gretchen Krause," the woman said, giving Mo a crisp handshake. "I'm the half that does all the heavy lifting."

"Gretch is a genius with sets and costumes," Madam T said. "She has a gift with color and fabric. And Ms. Quinn edits our marvelous community newspaper."

"Mo Knows," Gretchen acknowledged with a wink.

"We were just discussing that noise I heard the night someone killed our poor, dear Charlie," Madam T said.

"Has she shared her theory on alien invaders yet?" Gretchen asked.

"You stop that!" her partner protested. "We both saw the UFO that night on Picnic Point. You just refuse to admit it."

"She never misses an episode of *X - Files*," Gretchen said.

"Did you hear anything unusual that night? Mo directed at Gretchen.

"I never said it was a flying saucer," Madam T persisted. I don't know what it was. But it wasn't of this earth."

"I didn't hear a thing," Gretchen said. "I was already asleep."

"I know who made it," Madam T said, looking directly at Mo.

"The flying saucer?" Gretchen prodded.

"No! The noise I heard that night."

"Who?" Mo leaned forward.

"The monster who murdered Charlie."

"Do you have any idea who that might be?"

"A lot of people hated Charlie for what he was." Her voice trembled.

"Charlie was a homo," Gretchen said, reaching out to

pat Madam T's knee. "But I'm sure most of the good, god-fearing, queer-hating people of Mitchell didn't know."

Sobs shook Madam T's narrow, bony shoulders. Gretchen put an arm around her.

"I certainly didn't," Mo managed.

"Oh, they knew, all right," Madam T's said bitterly.

"And one of them killed Charlie as a hate crime?"

"I doubt it," Gretchen said at the same time that Madam T shrieked, "Yes! Yes! Yes!"

"Take it easy, love," Gretchen said, squeezing Nikki to her side.

The tremor in Nikki von Thoreaux' voice followed Mo out of the theater and into the afternoon sunshine. It stayed with her as she walked back to the *Doings*, carrying a tenuous motive for Charlie's murder.

. . . .

Bruce Randall was sitting on Viola Meugard's desk when Mo walked in. Vi had been the *Doings'* office manager since the invention of movable type. Her desk at the front of the building afforded her a front-row seat for the passing parade. She was laughing, her head thrown back, her mouth wide open, her eyes squeezed shut. Bruce had that effect on people. He was the size and shape of an adolescent grizzly bear and nearly as hairy, with stringy black hair and bushy black beard starting to pepper with gray.

Mo was always glad to see Bruce, the ad salesman she had inherited when she took on the *Doings*. He didn't spend much time around the office, preferring to go out and "grab 'em by the ears and twist until they buy an ad."

Vi struggled to pull herself together when she saw Mo come in. "Garnish his wages," she said, gasping for breath.

"That's what they do when you sue a parsley farmer," Bruce said for Mo's benefit.

"Go on," Mo said. "There's never just one."

"If you arrest a mime, does he have the right to make a noise?"

Vi whooped and fell back in her chair.

"If it's tourist season, why can't we shoot them?"

"You all through?"

"Can you be a closet claustrophobic?"

The phone rang. Vi clapped her hands over her mouth. Bruce leaned over and snatched up the receiver.

"*Doings*. This is Randall. Yeah. Yeah. Now why is that, Phil?" Bruce rolled his eyes. "Yeah. I heard what you said. I just don't understand it. You run two pages with us every week. Uh-huh. Uh-huh. It's your call, Phil. But you're going to have a tough time getting folks to clip coupons from your radio ad. Yeah. Right. I'll catch up with you next week."

He hung up. "Suck egg mule," he said.

"Phil Cranley?"

"The same. He's pulling his double truck this week."

"Did he say why?"

"Nope. And neither did the other four who pulled their ads."

"They're waiting to see what you write about Charlie," Vi said.

"What could I possibly write about Charlie that would hurt any of them?"

"The truth," Bruce said. "If he was murdered, it could be bad for business around here."

Mo fought a sudden urge to ball her fists and pound the desk. "They're pressuring me not to print something, and I don't even have the story yet to print."

"Sounds like one of them Catch-22 deals to me," Bruce said.

Mo took a deep breath. "Now what?"

"Now you do your job, I do my job, and Vi keeps the

paper running, like always. Folks will stay out for a week, maybe two, figure out they've got no place else to go, and put their ads back in. We will, as the Dead say, get by."

He stood up and stretched his big frame. "Meanwhile, I'm going to get out and scrounge for whatever pennies might still be on the table. I'll catch you ladies on the flip side."

Mo took her phone messages and retreated to her desk across the room. She knew when she took the job that she'd be in for long hours and short pay, but nobody told her when she traded in the big city for life in small-town, rural Wisconsin, that she'd end up in the middle of a murder investigation.

He did it because he loves me, Mo told herself as she eased to a stop at the highway 26 turnoff and waited for a gap in oncoming traffic.

He did it because he's concerned for my safety, she told herself. He raised his voice ("I am NOT yelling," he had insisted) because, under all that male bluster, he was a little scared for me.

Maybe he had a right to be.

Now!

She gunned the car across the narrow gap onto the country road. This route let her avoid going all the way in to Fond du Lac and up along the western shore of Lake Winnebago but subjected her to the possibility of getting stuck behind a manure spreader, school bus, or other rolling road block.

Even on her best mornings, Mo Quinn was not a patient driver. This was not one of her best mornings.

She hated leaving the house upset, with Doug still seething, angry words hanging in the air and no time for the calming down, the resurfacing of reason, the apologies and embraces.

"Your own publisher is trying to chase you off a story!" Doug had rolled the newspaper into a tight baton and walked a tight circle around the kitchen. "Mo, this is nuts! And you're nuts if you think you can continue to play editor for a lunatic like that!"

If only he hadn't said 'play.' If only he had used another word.

"It may seem like play to you, Douglas Stennett, but it's my career."

"I don't care what it is, it's gotten way out of hand, Mo. Good Lord…"

"Frankly, I think editing a community newspaper is every bit as important as tracking 'market fluctuations' every time Alan Greenbacks sneezes."

He hated it when she threw Alan Greenspan up at him—especially when she called him "Greenbacks" or "Greenbucks" or "Daddy Warspan."

"Yes, indeed!" he had said softly. "Breaking the big story on Bessie Mae Harper visiting her niece up in Osseo for the weekend is pretty damn significant stuff."

"It's important to Bessie Mae Harper!"

"So, for Bessie Mae Harper, you're going to drive all the way up to Oshkosh to talk to the last poor sap who tried to put up with that lunatic's ranting?"

If only he hadn't said "poor sap." If only he had used another phrase.

She couldn't even eat the beautiful eggs Benedict he had gotten up early to make for her. How could she eat, with her stomach roiling and her blood pounding? She wondered if he'd been able to eat after she left. He didn't even like eggs Benedict.

She slowed through Rosendale, a notorious speed trap, and tried to lose herself in a local talk show on the radio.

Morgan Winslow, the "last poor sap" to edit the *Mitchell Doings,* had landed a job as a general assignment reporter for the *Oshkosh Eagle Beacon.*

"To tell you the truth," he told her as they sat in the crowded employees' cafeteria, "the job paid so lousy, getting canned was almost a relief."

She had to lean over the little table to hear him over the noise. With the day's paper put to bed, most of the editorial staff was unwinding with a last cup of coffee before heading home.

Winslow was a large man who sat hunched over, shoulders up, head bent forward, perhaps the result of too many hours sitting at a keyboard, squinting at a screen. Would she end up slouching like that? He wore a corduroy jacket, white T-shirt, and grungy Levis. The smell of stale tobacco hung on him.

Winslow was already long gone when Mo took the job. Arthur Samuelson, the editor of the nearby *Riverpark Courier Gazette,* another in the Pierpont "chain" of community weeklies, had edited both papers for four or five months, until Pierpont had gotten around to hiring a new editor.

"I must say, though, that the way he did the deed struck me as being a trifle callous."

"How's that?"

"The first I knew I'd been canned was when I fanned open the week's compendium of typos and glanced at the masthead, which had a little strip of white space where the line 'Editor: Morgan Winslow' should have been. Pierpont had made poor Viola get out the Exacto knife and perform an editorectomy."

"Why?"

"In a nutshell, I pissed off an advertiser. The advertiser put the screws to Pierpont. Pierpont put the boot to me. Done deal."

"Which advertiser?"

"Boldt Enterprises, premiere pickle packers and processors."

"And the second largest employer in the county."

"Indeed. And a big advertiser in what we refer to in reverent tones as the Pierpont Family of Newspapers."

"What did you do to get them mad?"

"Reported the truth. Ah, but you want details."

"Please."

"Dogs all over town started to get sick. Very mysterious. Doc Zimmerman said they were being poisoned, a mild toxin of some sort, enough to make them up-chucky, but not dead. About that time, Dilly Nurtleman came in with slime all over his pants cuffs. He said he'd been mucking around one of the drainage pipes that empties into the Oshnaube. I went to look, and sure enough, the pipe was spewing slime bubbles. Apparently, dogs found the bubbles tasty, lapped them up, and got pukey sick."

"Where were the bubbles coming from?"

"Care to make a guess?"

"The Boldt pickle processing plant."

Morgan granted her a sly, gentle grin, a quick nod. "That's what I figured, too. But a journalist must never assume. I needed proof—which in this case was real easy to come by. I just followed the drainage pipe to its source."

"Did Pierpont try to stop you from printing the story?"

"I knew better than to give him the chance. About a year before, he'd gotten his moist little mitts on a feature I wrote on a farmer who claimed he'd gotten sick when the wind shifted, and the pesticide he was spraying on his fields blew back in his face. I didn't say the stuff made him sick. I simply said he said it made him sick. And I didn't mention the name of the pesticide or the store where he bought it. But I figured folks ought to have some warning if there was even a chance they were using something on their fields that could hurt them.

"But Pierpont passed a stone when he read it. He said Jeff Meeks down at the Co-op—I'm sure you've met Mr. Meeks by now—wouldn't like it. The Co-op being our biggest advertiser, what Mr. Meeks didn't like didn't get in the paper. He said he'd can me if I ran it."

"And you pulled it?"

"Hell, no. I ran it. Pierpont had the piece pulled at the printing plant and pasted in a house ad. Like a damn fool, I didn't quit right then. I could have saved myself another year of grief. You want some more coffee?"

"This round's on me."

Mo got the refills. They pretty much had the cafeteria to themselves now.

"Thanks." Winslow doctored his coffee with three spoons of sugar and two plastic containers of nondairy creamer. When he finished, he looked up and smiled at her. "This is about poor old Charlie, isn't it?"

"How'd you figure that?"

"It wasn't tough. I read that he'd died. You're investigating, and old Pisspot doesn't want you to. Right?"

"Right. He says we'd look bad if it turns out to be an accident, like the Sheriff says."

Winslow shrugged, took a slurp of coffee, set his mug down. "But you'd like to know for sure."

"He didn't die from eating Boldt pickles."

Winslow snorted. "Pisspot just may have met his match in you," he said.

"Thanks."

"So, who would have killed him? Saying somebody did."

"You know Charlie. Everybody in town loved him."

"But…"

"But, he had an argument with a mystery man the night he died."

Winslow hmmmmed.

"What don't I know about him?" she pressed. "Any skeletons in Charlie Connell's closet?"

Winslow took a long swallow of coffee. "Christ, I wish you could still smoke in here," he said. Then he leaned forward, his already maddeningly quiet voice becoming even quieter.

"Oh, old Charlie's had a skeleton," he said. "And it's a beaut."

Mo felt her pulse quicken. Winslow studied his hands, which were cupping his coffee mug. He shook his head, took a breath, looked down again. He said something that sounded like "Ax norm poppins…"

"What?"

"His hand reached for his inside coat pocket but then dropped back onto the table. "You talked to Norb Hopkins, right?"

"Yeah."

"Talk to him again. Ask him why Charlie had to stop helping out with the wrestling team."

"What?"

"Just ask him. That's all I'll give you."

"Is it because Charlie was a homosexual?"

Winslow nodded. "You'd have to say that had something to do with it," he said, getting to his feet. "I wish you well. I really do. If you can hack it working for Pisspot, more power to you."

With that he turned and walked across the empty cafeteria, leaving Mo with lots of time on the drive back to Mitchell to speculate on the dark mystery in Charlie's past. Doug got up from his desk, walked through the house and out onto the screened porch. He still wasn't used to being home during the day, and it made him feel vaguely uncomfortable, even guilty. Everyone else in the world had places to go and things to do. Only invalids and old people stayed home all day.

Maybe that was why he had unloaded on Mo that morning.

. . . .

He went into the kitchen. The eggs Benedict were congealing in the sink. He crammed the mess down the disposal and let the metal teeth grind it down.

The phone rang. Let it. He hated the phone.

It rang a second time and then a third.

"Hi." Mo's professional voice on the answering machine. "We can't come to the phone right now. When you hear the beep, you know what to do."

"Hello?" A girl's voice, scared. "I need to talk with Mrs. Quinn. It's very important." A pause. "Hello?" He heard a male voice, also young, in the background, but couldn't make out what he was saying. "I'll call back," the girl said. "Goodbye."

Frowning, Doug replayed the message, straining to make out what the male was saying.

He went back to the den and tried to lose himself in his work, but the fear in the girl's voice and the anger in Mo's that morning both stayed with him.

She got home late, having put in the sort of day that makes community newspaper editors consider switching to an easier line of work, like bullfighting. He was at the computer in his office. When he heard her behind him, he got up.

"What are you working on?" She nodded toward the screen.

"Steve Carlson for Rick Wise. Maybe the fifth or sixth worst trade in history. No Broglio for Brock, certainly, or Pappas for Robinson, but right in there with Gaylord Perry for Sudden Sam McDowell."

"Brock hadn't done a thing for Chicago," she said, smiling. "It looked like a good deal for my Cubbies at the time."

Statistical analysis of major league baseball trades was the second great passion of his life—after her, he insisted.

"What's this?"

Doug had spotted the package in Mo's hand.

"Peace offering."

"I should be giving you a present. I was a jerk."

"I agree totally. And I'm a saint to put up with you."

She slid into his tentative embrace. His lips were cool against hers. After the careful kiss, she handed him the package.

"Open it."

His smile was quizzical as he tore open the wrappings— another salvaged section of color comics from the Sunday paper. He shook his head as he turned the slender book over in his hands and lovingly opened the cover to the title page.

"I haven't had one of these in my hands in years," he said softly.

The book that was transporting him back to boyhood was *The Secret Panel,* one of the early *Hardy Boys Mysteries.*

"This is an original," he murmured, rubbing a finger over the raised type.

"To replace the one you lost."

Early in their relationship, Doug had told her about the book a friend had given him, the book that ignited his interest in reading after several years of being a chronic "underachiever" in school. He had stayed up all night, struggling to work through the book. Then he read every other Hardy Boy Book he could find, discovering the joy of the printed page. That first book had been *The Secret Panel.*

It was the first really personal revelation he had granted her. She had started to fall in love with him from that moment.

"I just thought you might need a good book to read tonight while I'm out."

"Do you have to? Tonight?"

"I've been putting Heiss off for weeks."

"I know, but I was hoping…"

"What were you hoping?" She pressed against him,

bending her head up to his kiss. "I won't be gone all night," she said when they broke the kiss.

"You'd better not be. What do you want to do about dinner?"

"That's my second surprise." She picked up the sack she had set on the table and which Jack Roosevelt had been rubbing with his muzzle. "I stopped at the Boston Market on my way back. Meatloaf with tomato sauce, baby red potatoes, mixed peas and carrots."

"I don't deserve you!"

. . . .

She met William Heiss out at the old church by the river  where, five years before, Heiss had been instrumental in establishing the Mitchell Historical Society Museum. When the church had come up for sale, Heiss headed a fundraising drive to buy it for the Society. He would have fallen considerably short had not Mrs. Wallace Pierpont come forward at the eleventh hour to put up the majority of the money.

Heiss filled the old church with exhibits and photographs of the town from the turn of the century. A fine amateur photographer named Henry Schubert had done an especially nice job of documenting cheese-making practices at the old Mitchell Cheese Company, which had ceased production in 1984, a victim of economies of scale and tightening environmental protection laws.

Other Schubert photos revealed the evolution of many of the town's buildings. El Mondo had been The Temple Vaudeville House, for example, The Country Store was a black smithy and livery, and Charlie's Mitchell Diner housed a local brewery, Mitchell's Mighty Fine Ale.

But the real tour de force of the Mitchell Historical Society Museum and the source of Bill Heiss' greatest pride was the mural that stretched across the inside back wall. Heiss had commissioned an itinerant artist named Randall Jarred to paint the tableau. It began on the far left with a depiction of the Winnebago who inhabited the area before the first whites "discovered" it, ran through the days when the passenger train made regular stops in Mitchell on its way from Chicago up to Minneapolis/St. Paul, encompassed the first automobile to appear on local roads and the development locally of a revolutionary method for baling and binding hay, through the coming of the pickle factory, the Co-op, the printing plant, and, finally, Pierpont's Phenomenal Fun Zone and Amusement Park.

Tucked in to the right corner of the mural, Father Julian Francis Thomas emerged from the door behind the altar to say the mass, as he had done for 34 years, until his death at the age of 74 in 1981, the last year the old building had served as a church.

"Poor Jarred worked all through the winter to get it done in time for the dedication," Heiss explained after finishing his scene-by-scene explication. "All we had in here was a little space heater, and he had to come over to the Diner every half hour or so to warm his hands enough to grip his brushes. He said he was afraid the paint was going to freeze."

Heiss talked steadily, pausing only to make sure Mo was getting everything. He was a small man, in shirtsleeves and unbuttoned vest, a few shocks of gray hair sticking up like pale hay on his nearly bald skull. He wore half lenses perched on his nose.

"Why don't we look at the collection of stringed instruments next?" he suggested, moving away from the mural.

But Mo returned to the photograph of the brewery.

"Where did they store the beer?" she asked, peering intently at the little building.

The curator beamed. "Good question! And one that might have gone unanswered had not the cable television people dug where they shouldn't have. A worker literally fell into the subbasement. It was an archeological gold mine of old bottles and beer-making paraphernalia. I've got some of it over here, if you'd like to see it."

"What about the subbasement? Is it still in use?"

Heiss scratched his crop of gray straw. "I don't remember if they filled it in or just boarded it off. I can find out for you."

"I'd appreciate that."

He showed her the collection of beer bottles. Many of the older ones had odd shapes with square corners.

"Isn't this a beauty?" he said, handing her a green bottle with the squared corners and the Mitchell Brewery emblem, an eagle, raised on one surface.

"Gorgeous."

"They don't make them like that any more. A work of art."

Mo rolled the bottle over in her palm. She squeezed hard, feeling the raised edges dig into her skin.

"Shall we look at the fiddles and guitars now?"

"Sure." She handed the bottle back but could still feel the imprint on her palm.

. . . .

When she finally got home, she found Doug upstairs in bed, Jack Roosevelt curled at his feet. Doug was reading his Hardy Boy mystery.

"This holds up pretty well," he said when she emerged from the bathroom. "Not great literature, but the plot steams right along."

"Better than stock market quotations?"

"They tell a story, too."

She snuggled in beside him.

"So, how was your interview?"

"Quite interesting, actually. Did you know the diner used to be a brewery?"

"Yeah? Mitchell had a brewery, huh?"

"A lot of the small towns did."

"Just listen to this prose. 'They headed back toward Bayport. Reaching an inlet, the boys went to a boathouse the Hardys rented for the Sleuth. It was a sleek-looking motorboat which they had bought with reward money received for solving a mystery about an old mill. Chet eyed his friends' boat a little enviously, but he knew they had earned it.' Great stuff, eh?"

"They had their own boat?"

"Yeah. And a roadster."

"Nancy Drew never got a boat."

He put the book down and peeled off his glasses. "Boys get all the neat toys," he said, grinning.

"You don't suppose the plot hinges on, oh, I don't know, a secret panel, maybe?"

"Hey! Don't spoil it for me!"

"Sorry."

"Have you started your book yet?"

"I did, actually, while I ate lunch. We're looking for a missing will."

"You don't suppose they'll find it in, oh, say, an old clock?"

She poked him. "Talk about giving away the plot."

"Sorry. So, what happened to the brewery?"

"Went broke, I guess, same as the cheese factory. They found a bunch of old beer-making stuff in a subbasement."

"Oh. I almost forgot. Repoz called. The coroner's report is in. He said you can call him in the morning if you want to."

"What else did he say?"

"That's it. Just call him in the morning."

"He didn't say anything about the report?"

"Nope."

"Maybe I should call him right now."

"I wouldn't. He said he was going to bed early."

He set his book on the nightstand, folded his glasses, and put them on top of the book. She rolled into his embrace. With the grace that comes only to lovers who have learned to trust, they made love and fell asleep in each other's arms.

. . . .

Sometime in the night, she woke to his gentle shaking.

"Mo? Honey?"

"Whassit?"

"I forgot to tell you about the other phone call. I let the machine take it."

"Who was it?"

"A girl. She said she needed to talk to you. It sounded urgent."

"What was her name?"

"She didn't say. She just said she'd call back. There was a boy's voice in the background. I think he surprised her, and that's when she hung up."

"How strange."

"Sorry I woke you. I was afraid I'd forget again."

"That's okay."

"Go back to sleep."

"I will."

Mo listened to Doug's breathing become deep and slow. She knew she wouldn't be able to sleep for a while, so she went downstairs and got a diet cran-raspberry from the refrigerator.

The message light on the kitchen phone blinked at her from the counter. She pressed the 'play last message' button, and the scared voice filled the darkened kitchen. Mo shivered. "Who are you?" she said when the recorder shut down. "What do you want to tell me?"

She sat at the counter, sipping her drink. Whatever it was, she felt certain it had something to do with Charlie's death.

"Males charge other males from the side or head on," Suzanne the Warrior Goddess said, "but they attack females from behind. They see you as prey."

Mo and the 16 other sweaty women in the "Impact on Your Model Mugger" class were cooling down from their workout with slow stretches while their leader summarized previous weeks' instruction.

The group was a mixture of young, fit women in colorful Lycra outfits that looked as if they had been spray-painted on and more sedentary types in raggy cutoffs and sweatshirts. There were also a couple of genuine wide-bodies, who made Mo feel positively svelte.

"That rules out the old kick-to-the-balls defense," Suzanne said, "but many lowlifes expect that anyway. If they do come at you from the front, you might be better off taking a shot to the knee or shin."

Suzanne spoke softly. From her tone of voice, she might have been describing nothing more violent than whipping egg whites into stiff peaks.

After Mo had been mugged on her way from her

office to the parking structure in downtown Chicago after working late one night, she had promised herself that she would learn martial arts. She had tried karate and tae kwan do, but it seemed to her that they would work only if the attacker stuck to the script.

When Mo saw the "Mugger" class advertised in a university noncredit catalog, she decided she wanted the structured physical activity and the excuse to drive to Madison once a week.

"Our strength is in our legs," Suzanne said, smacking her thighs with her open hands, "not in our upper arms. So don't try to punch your way out of trouble. Fight with your legs."

They don't teach that in martial arts, Mo reflected, feeling tightness in her right hip as she leaned into a leg stretch.

"If you have to use your hands, use the heel of your palm and ram the chin or nose. If he's already too close for that, claw his eyes."

Mo was still somewhat in awe of Suzanne. She was a big woman, but when she moved, nothing shook. And she moved with astonishing quickness and an economy that struck Mo as nothing short of beautiful.

"Your attacker will underestimate you," Suzanne said softly. "He'll figure you for a helpless female. Surprise is your best weapon. Strike fast. Adrenalin will only carry you for 30 seconds. Disable the bastard and run like hell. You don't want to be around when he gets his second wind.

"Geoff, anything to add?"

Geoff stood off to the side, arms folded over chest. He was a huge, powerfully built man, and he wore a grotesque facemask. He stared at them, eyes cold and menacing behind the eyeholes in the mask. Mo didn't like Geoff. She wasn't supposed to. He was the attacker they were learning to defend against.

"I guess Geoff has nothing to add," Suzanne said with a smile. It was an ongoing joke. Geoff never spoke. He did occasionally grunt.

"Okay. Last stretch. Nice and slow. Good. Good. Remember, in street fighting, there are no rules. All together now."

"FIGHTING DIRTY WINS!" they chanted.

Suzanne rewarded them with a smile. "See you next week. Stay out of trouble. But if trouble finds you, you know what to do. You are in the cult of Suzanne, the Warrior Goddess!"

"How about a triple mocha latte, to replace all the calories we just burned up?" Kaye asked as they reached the door together.

"Can't," Mo said, smiling. "I've got to see a man about a murder."

"I read about that." Kaye held the door for Mo. "The Madison papers say it was an accident."

"That's what the Sheriff is saying."

"But you don't think so?"

"I'm going to go find out what the coroner has to say."

Kaye made a face. "What a grizzly business," she said.

"But no problem for a warrior goddess."

"Absolutely. Where's your car?"

"I'm going to walk. It's such a pretty morning, and it's just on the other side of the square."

"Okay. See you next week?"

"Wouldn't miss it."

"Fighting dirty wins."

"Fighting dirty absolutely wins."

Madison had everything, Mo reflected as she walked up State Street: wonderful and unique restaurants, first run and "arty" movie houses, funky used bookstores, somehow surviving in the shadow of the immense super chains, and more places to get coffee and fresh bagels than a human being could exhaust in a lifetime.

Despite the best efforts of the "developers" to destroy it and the satellite malls to strangle it, the six blocks of State Street linking the university with the Capitol Square were still vibrant. And two beautiful lakes bordered the downtown isthmus.

Madison had everything. Everything except a parking space.

As she got closer to the Capitol, scruffy students with backpacks gave way to men and women in suits and in a hurry. A bearded street musician picked out an intricate progression on his acoustic guitar, a black shaggy mongrel lay asleep in the open guitar case. "I MAKE MY LIVING BY MY MUSIC," a hand-printed sign propped up on the case announced, "PLEASE BE GENEROUS." Mo dropped two dollars in the case.

"Thanks, babe," the man said.

"Spare change," a vacant-eyed man challenged, thrusting a hand out. Mo gave him a dollar.

She circled the Capitol, bicyclists weaving in and out among the flitting cars and huffing buses. Sun filtered through the trees. Squirrels scampered across the sloping lawn. Mo wished she had time to linger. She and Doug would have to make a trek to Madison soon. Maybe a picnic on the Capitol square lawn, a browse through Shakespeare's used books, a beer on the Union Terrace.

She walked the two blocks to the City County Building, which housed the County Sheriff's Department. Sheriff Repoz himself met her in the waiting area.

"What do you do, run here from Mitchell?" he said by way of greeting.

"Self defense class."

Repoz threw up his hands. "I surrender," he said.

He was a short, compact man with short-cropped, flint-gray hair, fierce blue eyes, and a reddish gray brush mustache, neatly trimmed.

"We could have done this on the telephone," he said, leading her to his office.

"I was in the neighborhood."

Sheriff Repoz led her through a maze of cubicles and down a hallway to his office. He waved her into a chair before taking his place in a high-backed chair behind a huge desk that had not so much as a post-it note marring its polished oak surface. He nearly disappeared in the large chair, looking, Mo thought, like a child playing office. Mo took a straight-backed chair facing the desk.

"You can't publish this yet," he said without preamble. "Agreed?"

"I don't sign blank checks, Sheriff."

"Look." Repoz leaned forward and put his clasped hands on the bare desk. "I'm giving you this because it's your story, your town."

"I appreciate that. What can you give me on the record?"

"Lacerations and contusions. A blow to the head, which could have killed him."

"Consistent with a fall down the stairs?"

"Could have been."

"But you don't think so."

"We're still on the record, right?"

"Right. Lacerations and contusions. What else?"

"Time of death between midnight and 4:00 a.m. Mother discovered the body, as you know, at about 4:45, when Charlie didn't answer his morning wake-up call."

"Not very helpful."

"Not very."

"Wasn't he last seen around 10 p.m.?"

"You've been busy."

"Just doing my job, Sheriff."

"The guy who runs the video rental places him outside the diner, in the rain, around 10:00."

"With a mysterious stranger."

"Right. With a mysterious stranger."

"Any idea who the mysterious stranger was?"

Repoz pursed his lips and shook his head. "We know that Charlie had had a few beers. He had a blood alcohol of .07."

"Charlie and the mysterious stranger argued, and the mysterious stranger came back later and killed him."

Repoz shrugged. "Could be. But what's the motive? Robbery, maybe?"

"Charlie's mother says the bank opened specially for Charlie so he could deposit the receipts on Saturdays. There wouldn't have been any cash lying around."

Mo thought she saw surprise register on the sheriff's face for an instant. "We'll check that," he said.

"Anything else?"

"This has to be off the record or not at all. The killer would be the only one to know about it."

Mo closed her notebook, put it on the desk between them, and put her pencil on top of the notebook.

"As if you won't remember every word."

"Off the record. You have my word."

"Okay. To get the lacerations and contusions Charlie had, he would have had to get up and throw himself back down those stairs four or five times."

"What else?"

"The mark on his head where he was hit."

"What kind of mark?"

"Some sort of pattern. We're studying pictures to try to figure out what it is."

"So you're saying somebody hit him with something that left a funny mark and then threw him down the stairs to make it look like an accident."

"I'm saying it could have happened that way."

"Why are you telling me this?"

Repoz smoothed his mustache. "I'm telling you because you need to know that we're probably dealing with a killer. You need to be very careful." He stood up. The interview was over.

"I appreciate that." She stood, leaning over the desk to shake his hand.

After she left the City County Building, she quickly walked the four blocks to St. Raphael's for noon mass. Ordinarily, she wouldn't have considered going to mass still grubby from a workout, but the cavernous, almost empty old cathedral granted her anonymity.

She took a place in a pew halfway up the long aisle. The hollow thwack of her wooden kneeler cracking the stone floor echoed through the church. Mo glanced around, but the few elderly supplicants dotting the pews took no notice. She eased onto her knees, made the sign of the cross, and waited for her heart and thoughts to quiet.

I am so scared, she told God and herself.

She wondered if it would be all right to pray for a revelation about Charlie. But wasn't that the same as praying to win a game? It had long ago occurred to her that, if members of her Immaculate Heart of Mary field hockey team were praying for victory, chances were good that the players for Saint Peter's were praying just as hard. What was God supposed to do?

St. Peter's must have prayed harder, because they won four years in a row. She decided to pray for a clear head and sound judgment, which is what the Sisters told her to do before a test.

The rustlings of people standing up roused her from her thoughts. A short, slight priest, who must have been pushing the Diocesan retirement age of 75, had entered from the side door behind the altar. Mo stood, carefully easing the kneeler up.

"In the name of the Father," the priest intoned, bringing his open hand to his forehead, "and of the Son, and of the Holy Spirit."

"Amen."

The familiar rhythms of the liturgy carried her.

"I understand why you go to mass on Sunday," Doug had told her early in their marriage. "You think you have to. But why do you subject yourself to that nonsense on weekdays?"

"I don't go because I have to," she'd snapped, angry with herself for failing to find the words to explain her faith to him. Since then, Doug had seemed to tolerate her religiosity but had never shown any curiosity about her beliefs.

The Gospel reading this day was one of her favorites, the account of Jesus walking on the water. The disciples had been terrified, and Peter had demanded that Jesus prove Himself by bidding Peter to walk on the water, too. So walk already, Jesus said. Peter took a few halting steps but then took his eye off Jesus, becoming conscious of the waves, and immediately began to sink.

Mo thought about poor old Peter while the priest recited the prayers of consecration. Impetuous Peter, the Rock upon which Christ built the church. Jesus' special friend, but the one who denied Him three times the night before the agony of the cross. He must have carried the memory of that betrayal with him to his own martyrdom.

For that matter, it occurred to her, even Judas, who sold

Christ for 30 pieces of silver, had been a friend, the one entrusted with the common purse.

Betrayed by a friend. The thought lodged in her mind.

"Through Him, with Him, and in Him, in the unity of the Holy Spirit. All honor and glory is yours, Almighty Father. Forever and ever."

"Amen." Mo's quiet voice disappeared into the cavernous church.

She had been looking for Charlie's enemies. But could a trusted friend have murdered him?

The sibilant shuffling of shoes on stone called her back. She stood and took her place in line, moving slowly forward to receive the sacred body—what Doug called the "poker chip." She stepped forward, hands extended and cupped, and looked into the rheumy eyes of the old priest.

"The body of Christ."

"Amen."

She felt the coolness of his hand as he placed the wafer in hers. She stepped aside, pinched the disk with her thumb and forefinger, and put it into her mouth, wetting her fingertips and blotting stray flecks of host on her palm and putting her fingers to her tongue. She made the sign of the cross, turned, and walked down the side aisle, feeling the wafer dissolve in her mouth.

Kneeling again, she watched the priest clear the altar—"doing the dishes," Doug called it—and prayed for guidance.

"The mass is ended."

"Thanks be to God."

"Go in peace to love and serve the Lord."

"Amen."

"And we do that best," the old priest added, "by serving one another."

Amen to that, Mo thought, collecting her purse. As she

emerged into the brightness of the early afternoon, she began to compose a list of Charlie Connell's friends so she could sift through them for a potential betrayer.

Mo had talked to Wallace J. Pierpont exactly twice. The third meeting could be the last, she reflected as she drove out to the amusement park.

She had no intention of being run off a job she loved, but she also had no intention of spiking a potential story because some advertiser didn't like it.

Her first session with Pierpont had been her job interview at his office in the 'farmhouse' on the hill overlooking the amusement park.

"Who's your favorite writer?" Pierpont had asked immediately. "You read any Zane Grey?"

"Sure," she said, scanning her memory banks. "*Riders of the Purple Sage.*"

Pierpont leaned back with a satisfied nod. "Grey is one of the most underrated writers in the English language," he said. "Don't you agree?"

He didn't wait for a reply, launching into a discourse on Zane Grey. He might have been a character out of a Zane Grey novel himself, Mo reflected, or at least central casting's idea of what the rich ranch owner in a Zane

Grey novel should look like: a grizzled, ropey old man, his narrow face topped with an impressive sweep of silver hair. He wore dress shirt, bolo tie, and khaki work pants, the fabric weary beyond all wrinkling.

Pierpont had stopped talking and was watching her.

"Uh, Grey really captured the spirit of the West," she stammered.

"Didn't he?" Pierpont hopped up and strode to the floor-to-ceiling bookshelf, where he snatched down a volume without having to hunt for it. "Listen to this," he said, turning back to Mo, the book falling open in his hand. "Listen to this!"

He read for several minutes, then snapped the volume shut with satisfied finality and resumed his place behind his desk. "So," he said, "you want the job, or what?"

"Excuse me?"

"Do you want the job? That's what we're talking about, isn't it?"

"Well, yes, but…"

"The lady you worked for at the *Trib* said they hated to lose you." Pierpont snatched up notepad and pencil and scrawled something. "Here's what I can pay you." He tossed the pad across the desk to her. "If you work out, we'll talk about bumping it up."

Pierpont hadn't amassed his wealth by overpaying the help, Mo noted.

"I need to call my husband. We didn't know you'd be offering…"

"That doesn't count your fringes," he said. "You get damn good medical and dental. No shrinks, though. Don't believe in them."

"But I still…"

"Are you holding me up for more money?" Pierpont scowled. Then he grinned. "Good for you. If you don't think you're worth much, why should anybody else think so?"

He snatched back the pad, rubbed out the original figure, penciled in another. "That's as high as I can go," he said, tossing the pad back in her direction. "Deal?"

Mo had taken a deep breath. When they had left Chicago, she had told Doug that, more than anything, she'd like to edit a community newspaper. Now she was getting her chance. "Deal," she said without looking at the figure on the pad.

Thus Mo had accepted long hours of underpaid servitude, intense anxiety, a crash course in small town psychology, and more satisfaction than she had ever imagined a job could give.

She got phone calls and notes from her new boss, and she glimpsed him once in his khakis and railroad engineer's cap, sweeping up the Phun Zone Arcade, but her publisher never summoned her back to his office on the hill, and he appeared at her office only once, late one Tuesday night as Mo struggled to get the front page of the *Doings* laid out. Pierpont had barged in past Viola's vacant reception desk and into the back room, where Mo was laboring over the light table.

"Don't let me slow you up. Ned's waiting on you over at the plant. I don't make any money when the presses aren't running, you know."

He plunked down on the high stool next to hers and rustled open the white bakery bag he was carrying. "You want chocolate glaze or raspberry fill?"

"Raspberry." She kept her eyes on the half-constructed page in front of her.

"This is the last time you'll ever have to use the scissors and waxer," Pierpont said. He took a huge bite out of a chocolate glazed and passed her the bag.

"How's that?" For a moment she thought she might be getting fired.

"We're going Macintosh next week," Pierpont managed around a mouthful of donut. "Word processing, layout, and full pagination. The works. We'll be right up there with the big boys."

"But I've never…"

He waved half a donut at her to silence her. "I'm having the boxes set up Friday night. You, Vi, and Bruce can come in over the weekend and figure out how to make them work. How's that suit you?" Pierpont shoved the rest of the donut into his mouth and grinned. He had a speck of chocolate on his chin.

Mo put down the column of text she had been about to wax and turned to face her boss. "That suits me right down to the ground," she said.

"That's the stuff that makes admirals," Pierpont said, licking the chocolate off his fingers.

The memory would have made Mo smile as she parked and climbed the steps to the Pierpont house—if she weren't dreading the prospect of facing down her strong-willed employer.

This time Pierpont didn't offer her a donut.

"What can I do for you?" he asked without getting up from the big chair behind the desk

"I'm more interested in what you're trying to do to me."

"Sit down." He gestured toward the same chair she had been hired in. "Coffee?"

Pierpont motioned toward the assistant standing in the doorway. "Get us some coffee, Woodrow.

"Want anything in it?" he directed at Mo.

"No."

"Good. If you're going to drink coffee, drink coffee. If

you want Ovaltine, have Ovaltine. So. You're here about Charlie, yes?"

"Yes."

"Good. What have you decided to do?"

"There's nothing to decide. I'm going to get the story and write it as well as I can."

"Are you? And what is the story?"

"I don't know yet."

"No conspiracy theories?"

"Nope."

Woodrow appeared with two mugs of coffee.

"Here's a theory for you," Pierpont said when Woodrow had left. "Maybe I wasn't trying to chase you off the story at all. Maybe I wanted to see how you'd react. If you'd cut and run."

"You were testing me?"

Pierpont nodded.

"And I passed?"

"So far, so good."

"What test did Morgan Winslow fail?"

Pierpont leaned back in the chair. "I assume you've heard Mr. Winslow's version of events," he said.

"That's right."

"I would have assumed," he went on evenly, "that, as a journalist, you would have tried to get the other side of the story before making up your mind."

She sipped her coffee. It was something to do. "Good point," she conceded.

"Morgan Winslow was, among other things, dishonest."

The sun was almost down outside the broad window behind Pierpont, and his face was in shadow. He spread his hands, palms up. His eyes narrowed. "But you find it easier to believe the guy with the ax to grind."

"I believe what makes the most sense to me."

"You had me figured for an eccentric old coot. Isn't that right? He may be rich as Kennedy, but he's a couple of tacos short of a fiesta. Isn't that what everybody says about me?"

She met his gaze, reading there a calculating intelligence. "Something like that."

"That perception allows me to do exactly as I please"

The silence grew thick in the pale light of the last sun.

"Ms. Quinn," he said, rising from his chair and walking around the desk. "We're on the same side here. I'd like nothing better than to see the murderer of Charlie Connell brought to justice, and I want to read about it first in the *Mitchell Doings*." Taking her cue, she stood.

"Until that has been done," Pierpont added, "our little town will dwell in the shadow of fear and mistrust."

He let his hand rest lightly on Mo's sleeve. "Do whatever you need to do to find the killer," he said. "Expose him to the light. I believe that's what you were brought here to do."

Mo walked back down the hill fairly certain of just two things. A lot of people believed that Charlie Connell had been murdered, and some of them, including her boss, expected her to find out who did it.

Following Sabra Farnum's directions to the abandoned county landfill, Mo made her way out County YY "maybe a mile or two" (closer to four), recognized the collapsed barn at "the old Hoestedler place" (no Hoestedlers had lived there for three decades), found the farmhouse with the pond and the statue of the German shepherd by the back door and the Mary in the bathtub in the yard.

From there she took what she hoped was the right dirt road, a barely-discernible break in the grass, and bumped and rutted "about a mile" (two point four). She fought the temptation to turn back as she passed the sad sight of an abandoned farmhouse, the road narrowing until shrubs scratched the sides of the car.

She figured she had a lot better chance of getting information out of the mysterious Pete than Sheriff Repoz did. And if Repoz did get it, that meant the press in Madison would get it, too. This was her story, and she didn't want to read it first in the *Cardinal Herald.*

She passed the old landfill, long since topped off. The trailer should be close now. "You'll be able to tell the trailer from the old landfill because the landfill's a lot neater," Sabra had said.

Mo wrenched the steering wheel, sending the del Sol lurching into the bend in the road, and saw the trailer on the right. Sabra was right. It made the landfill look good.

The del Sol pitched to a stop. The engine ticked as it began to cool. Cicadas buzzed their electric chorus. A big dog barked in the distance.

Not too late to turn around and go back, she reminded herself.

Dear God, you've got the hairs on my head numbered, she prayed. I hope you're keeping track of the rest of me, too.

She took a deep breath, opened the car door, swung her legs out. She walked through dirt clods, tufts of weeds and twisted, rusted metal scraps, mounted the three rotting wooden steps and rapped on the aluminum door of the trailer.

A footfall. Mo fought the urge to turn and run. The trailer door wrenched open.

"Yeah?"

Mo realized she'd been expecting a fat woman in a tent dress. Instead, she took in the tiny woman in jeans and sleeveless T, age indeterminate, face weathered by more than time.

"I'm looking for Pete," Mo managed.

The woman had a long, narrow face and looked a little horsy.

"And who might you be?"

"Monona Quinn. I edit the *Doings*."

"Do you now?" She seemed to be sizing Mo up. "I guess Pierpont learned his lesson."

"How's that?"

"Never mind. Come on in. I've been after Pete to fix

the goddamn screen door, but I might as well ask the screen door to fix itself."

The woman held out a bony hand, the long, gnarly fingers splayed slightly. "My name's Carol," she said.

Mo gripped the hand, which felt like a bundle of wires in a rawhide sack.

"Sit down. Here. Hold on."

Carol grabbed a stool, sending whatever had been on top of it cascading, and thrust it at Mo. "Park yourself," she said. "I got iced tea."

"Thanks."

Carol went to the kitchen area and hoisted a pitcher out of the refrigerator.

"I guzzle this stuff by the gallon when it's hot," she said, returning with the pitcher and two glasses. "Sugar? Here. Taste it first and see if it needs it."

Mo took a tentative sip. The tea tasted vaguely grapey. "It's fine," she said.

"So. You got kids?" Carol sagged down into what was left of an old armchair, covered with a torn sheet. The chair swallowed her thin frame. She threw her legs over the side.

"No. No kids."

"Good for you. Career comes first, right?"

"My husband has two children from a previous marriage."

"Uh-huh. One in five. That's what Dr. Joy said the other day. One in five couples in America got some kind of infertility problem. She's the nice one. Joy Browne. The other one's a real pit bull."

Mo became aware of the low murmur of the radio on the counter.

"I listen to them all," Carol said. "Dr. Joy, Dr. Laura, Dr. Dean. On Saturdays I even listen to the dog and cat lady. You learn a lot."

"I imagine." Mo took another sip of the grapey tea.

"You're better off," Carol said.

"Excuse me."

"Not having kids. A royal pain in the ass, believe me." Her right hand flopped over the chair arm and groped for her glass of tea. Her bony fingers wrapped around the glass and hoisted it to her mouth. She drank off half of it, gave a satisfied sigh, and put the glass back on the floor.

"So, Pete's in some kind of trouble?"

"No, no," Mo said quickly.

"Mind if I smoke?" She was already dragging a pack of Camels from under the sheet.

"No. Go ahead."

"He's out someplace with the dog." Carol took a long drag and blew the smoke out her nose.

Mo hadn't seen her light the cigarette. That bothered her. It was like a movie that had been badly spliced. She wondered what else she was missing. Focus, she told herself.

"Now that he ain't working for Charlie, he spends a lot of time out walking with that dog. I guess they got a lot to talk about." Carol drank off the rest of her iced tea. "You want another shot?"

Mo's glass was still almost full. "No," she said. "Thanks."

"I keep after him to get another job, but he don't seem too eager. Hell, he's getting a free ride here. Why should he work, right? I know what Dr. Laura would say. She'd say I should throw the lazy mutt out, or at least charge him room and board, right?"

"I don't think I've ever heard Dr. Laura."

"Does this have something to do with old Charlie? Poor bastard. Died all alone in that diner, I heard."

"Yes. His mother found him."

Carol made a face. "Gross."

"I can't imagine anything worse," Mo said.

Carol pursed her lips around her cigarette and nodded. Smoke came out of the corners of her mouth. "I'm gonna get more iced tea," she said.

Mo took the opportunity to shift her weight and stretch her legs.

"And you figure," Carol said from the refrigerator, her back to Mo, "that maybe Pete had something to do with Charlie dying, right?"

Mo waited for Carol to return before answering. Carol set her glass on a table and flopped back in the chair.

"I'm just trying to piece together what happened," Mo said.

"He didn't," Carol said. "He's no saint, God knows. He's been in a few scrapes. But he didn't hurt that old queen, or anybody else. He wouldn't raise his hand to any creature. Hell, he won't even make the dog mind him.

"I don't mean..."

"When Bob was still around, he tried to teach Pete how to box. That was a joke. As if Bob knew a jab from a hook from his left nut. He'd take a poke at Pete, hit him right in the face, and Pete would just look at him. He wouldn't even hit back."

Carol squinted through a smoke cloud. The cigarette was down to a stub Mo would have thought too short to hold.

"If I thought he'd done it, I'd be the first to turn him in. Believe it, lady. I won't have any of that mess under my roof. But Pete didn't do anything."

"Where was he the night Charlie died?" Mo asked, wishing she didn't sound like dialogue from a bad cop show.

Carol snorted smoke from her nostrils. "He was here until Art Bell came on," she said. "I heard him go out after that, no doubt to play one of those role-play things with the other members of the coven." She laughed. "That stuff creeps me out."

Carol lit a fresh cigarette. Mo hadn't noticed what she did with the last one.

"What time would that be?"

"Art Bell comes on at midnight. It was probably closer to 1:00 when Pete left. I'd fallen asleep once and woke up when I heard him go out. He's a regular vampire. Roams until dawn and sleeps most of the day. It was tough on him, working the morning shift at Charlie's. But he did it."

"Where does he play this game?" Mo pressed.

"They usually meet at Brad Grover's. That's about half way back to town, off the road by the old Turville place."

"He biked?"

"You see any limos around here?" Carol drained her iced tea in three long gulps. "Bob took the pickup, goddamn his mangy thieving ass."

She looked up, suddenly attentive. Mo caught herself straining to hear whatever had gotten her attention.

"Hold on," Carol said. "You can talk to him yourself." She got up and walked to the door. "Leave the dog in the pen," she hollered before she had the door open. "We got company."

"I saw the car," a masculine voice said from outside.

A short, thin young man appeared in the doorway. He stopped and stared at Mo. He had his mother's face. A stocking cap covered his forehead, but his eyes and bone structure were all mama.

"This is Mrs. Quinn," Carol said, nodding toward Mo. "She does the newspaper. She's been asking about Charlie. I told her she might as well get it straight from the hyena's mouth."

"She thinks I done it?"

"She might have thought so when she got here," Carol said, nodding to Mo and winking. "But she knows better now. Ain't that right? Haven't I been setting you straight?"

He seemed like a shy, vulnerable kid, and Mo hoped she didn't have to bring him any more trouble than he already had.

"Take that ratty thing off in the house," Carol said. "I can't believe he wears that thing in the summer." She made a move to snatch the cap. Her son danced back, grinning. His mother darted forward, grabbing at him.

"No tickling!" he squealed.

He collapsed on the floor, howling as his mother fell on top of him.

"There now," Carol said triumphantly over her shoulder. "Didn't I tell you my Pete was a pussycat? He wouldn't hurt anybody. Not even that sad-assed old queen, Charlie Connell."

They stood up. Pete was only a shade taller than his mother.

"I'm glad to meet you," Mo said, extending her hand as she tried to imagine Pete as the mysterious stranger who had murdered Charlie Connell, or who had saved an old lady's dog, or both.

"You gonna give me the third degree?" Pete asked. He moved quickly to the refrigerator and brought out the iced tea pitcher, which had just a splash left.

"We need more tea, Ma," he said.

"Your hands busted?"

"I'll drink water."

Carol gave Mo a look and shrugged her shoulders.

"No third degree," Mo said.

Pete paced in the narrow space, glancing at Mo as if afraid she might pounce on him.

"You worked for Charlie, right?"

"Yump," Pete allowed. "Lemme have a ciggie," he said to his mother.

"You shouldn't smoke."

"Neither should you. Breathing your smoke will kill me anyway."

"I'm almost out."

"You can get more."

"What did you do for Charlie?" Mo broke in.

"Washed dishes. Bussed tables. Cleaned up."

"Something he won't do around here," Carol noted.

"What kind of guy was he to work for?"

Pete swigged his water and shrugged. "Okay," he said.

"Anybody who'd give Pete a job has to be an idiot," Carol said.

"Thanks." Pete glanced at her.

"You don't have a real impressive resume, baby love."

Mo waited while they went through what was clearly a well-practiced routine, with mother getting all the best lines.

"Tell me about Minnie," she said when there was a lull.

"Who?"

"The dog you rescued last winter."

"Oh, that. How'd you find out about that?"

"That's her job, knucklehead," Carol said.

"That was a very nice thing for you to do."

"He cried when he read about that lady and her dog in the paper," Carol told Mo.

Pete made a face. "I didn't cry," he said darkly.

"Excuse me, John Wayne."

"Mrs. Watkins would like to give you a reward," Mo told Pete.

"How much?" Carol asked immediately.

"I think we're talking candy, not cash."

"Terrific." Carol had a fresh cigarette again.

"She's very grateful," Mo told Pete.

"I didn't want the dog to starve."

"Did you see Charlie the night he died?"

"I told you he was at Brad's," Carol said.

"I was," Pete said, nodding. "I was at Brad's. You can ask him. You can ask his old lady."

"What time did you go to Brad's?"

"I dunno."

"It was after midnight," Carol said. "Art Bell was on."

"How about before that? You didn't go into town earlier?"

"Nope. No reason to."

"Well, then," Mo said, getting up. "I guess that's it. I'd love to get a picture of you with Mrs. Watkins and Minnie sometime."

"He don't like to get his picture took," Carol said at the same time Pete said, "Sure."

Nothing looked familiar to Mo as she bounced and pitched along the rutted road back toward town. She hoped she'd be able to find her way.

Either Pete and his mother were lying, she reflected, or Pete couldn't have been the man seen talking with Charlie outside the diner the night he died. And Sabra was right about Pete not seeming to be the killing kind.

But he did match the description, right down to the stocking cap. He knew Charlie, which also fit. And if he weren't the mystery man, Mo was still one mystery man short of a suspect.

At least she had the answer to one question, she reflected as the abandoned farmhouse came into view. Now she knew who had saved Minnie.

But that wasn't the mystery she really needed to solve.

"Talk to Norb Hopkins," Morgan Winslow had said. So talk to Norb Hopkins she did. Again.

But first she did her homework.

"I guess my editor won't mind if I let you graze a little bit," Joey Hasslebaum said as he cleared off a swivel chair and wheeled it up to one of the computer terminals dotting the floor of the *Cardinal-Herald* newsroom. "Especially if he doesn't find out about it."

"I really appreciate this."

"No problem. I get leads out of your paper all the time."

Joey had the back roads beat. Several times he had called Mo at the *Doings* to get names and numbers for features he wrote on local museums, festivals, and smalltown eccentrics.

Mo settled into the chair. Joey leaned over her. His fingers clattered the keys. He smelled of tobacco, coffee, and something else—essence of wet dog.

"You're in. I'll check back in a bit and see how you're doing."

After he left, she reflected on how quiet and neat—and smokeless!—the modern newsroom had become. She typed in "Mitchell" and scrolled a menu of stories, most relating to high school sports. She typed in "Connell, Charlie" and got all the stories about Charlie's death. She also got 11 matches for a Charles Connell who lived in Mt. Horeb and had something to do with the university alumni association.

She frowned at the screen. Poor Charlie had apparently only made the big city paper by dying. Where else could she look? Where the names might not be indexed?

She accessed the police reports for the six months leading up to the time when Charlie stopped helping with the wrestling team. Scrolling the lists would take hours. She copied a list, opened a word document, and pasted the list in. Then she ran the search function and typed in "Connell." She got several matches, none of them the right one.

She started working backward in time, copying and pasting lists and searching for "Connell." When she finally found what she wanted, her hand flew over her notepad.

"Find what you need?"

Joey Hasslebaum had walked up behind her without her realizing it.

"I did for a fact," she said, quickly closing down the program. "Thanks again." She gathered up notepad, pencil, and purse.

"No problem. Just remember me when you give your acceptance speech for the Pulitzer."

"I promise."

. . . .

"Best two falls out of three?" Coach Hopkins said when she appeared at his office door.

"Who won the first match?"

Hopkins almost smiled "Still haven't got Charlie buried yet?" he asked.

She took the seat across the desk, which seemed to have added another layer of debris, including a shriveled apple core. The coach cracked his knuckles, fished a sack of sunflower seeds off his desk, and, tipping his head back, poured seeds into his mouth.

"I came up with a couple more questions. I never seem to get everything I need the first time."

"Shoot." The coach settled back in his chair and laced his fingers behind his head.

"Thanks." Mo opened her notebook and leafed through the pages. "I appreciate your taking more time with me. I know how busy you are."

"Not busy enough," the coach said, picking up a paper cup and spitting seed husks into it. "They don't let us start practices for another two weeks."

"Have you found a good heavyweight?"

Hopkins looked surprised. "You follow high school wrestling, do you?"

"I edit the newspaper. I follow everything."

"I suppose. So, what are we following now?"

"Just a couple of loose ends to tie up. You told me Charlie continued to help out with the team after he graduated."

"That's right." Norb leaned back again, hands behind his head. His elbows jiggled slightly. "Charlie was like my good right hand," he said.

"But he quit in 1991. Why was that?"

"You know how Charlie was. Into a million and one things. He just got too busy."

"And that was the only reason why he stopped helping you?"

The elbow jiggling stopped. "I guess you already know the answer to that one," he said slowly, "or you wouldn't have asked."

"I'd like to hear your answer."

Coach leaned forward, the chair groaning under his weight. He picked up a cardboard coffee cup, looked at the inch of liquid in it, frowned, and put the cup back on the desk.

"I've had to tell a lot of boys they weren't good enough to wrestle for me," he said. "I've seen big, tough farm kids bust out crying. But telling Charlie was the toughest thing I've ever had to do in my entire career."

"Telling Charlie what?"

"To stay the hell away from my boys."

"Why'd you have to tell him that?"

The coach leveled a steady gaze at her. "I don't guess I have to tell you that," he said.

"Maybe you should. So there'll be no misunderstanding."

Coach looked down at his hands again and shook his head.

"Coach Hopkins," Mo said. "I'm certain Charlie Connell was murdered. I think we'd all like to know who murdered him. This community won't heal until we do."

"I don't see how digging all this up would help."

"I'm not sure it would," Mo conceded. "But it might."

"You can't print this."

"Is that the deal you had with Morgan Winslow?"

"I didn't have any deal with Morgan Winslow."

"I don't want to hurt Charlie's reputation."

"Yeah? And the media didn't want to hurt President Nixon's reputation, either."

"I'm no Woodward and Bernstein."

"Charlie got himself arrested up in Madison. I guess you found that out."

"Lewd conduct and public indecency."

"He told me it was all a misunderstanding. He said it was late, he had to take a piss, and he didn't think he'd make it back to his motel. So he whipped it out in public, and a cop saw him."

"He told you that?"

"I'm the one he called from the jail. He didn't want his mama to know."

"Who else knew?"

Norb shrugged. "I never told anybody," he said.

"This was in 1989, right?"

"If you say so."

"And Charlie helped out with the team for two more years."

The coach put his hands on his knees and leaned forward. He drew a long breath through his nose. "He exposed himself to one of my boys," he said to the floor. Seed husks dribbled out of the side of his mouth. "Frank Simpson. One of the best lightweights I ever coached. Charlie took him down into that basement of his and pulled his pants down."

"You're sure...?"

A single syllable, part bark, part laugh, escaped him, along with a few more seeds. "Frank said Charlie asked him to do you-know-what on his you-know-who," the coach said.

"What did Frank do?"

"Came and told me. When I went after Charlie, he cried like a baby. Said he knew it was wrong. Said it wouldn't happen again. I told him it sure as hell wouldn't. Told him if he ever came within a country mile of any of my boys again, I'd break him into pieces too small to sweep up."

"But you didn't tell anyone?"

Coach looked up, anger crowding his broad, pale face. "He didn't molest anybody." He said it the country way, "MO-lest."

"He tried to," Mo said softly. "Why didn't you turn him in?"

She heard the dripping of the shower down the hall. The coach drew in more air through his nose and blew it out of his mouth in short puffs. "You're not from around here," he finally said.

"How did Morgan Winslow find out?"

"You'd have to ask him that."

"I will."

"God damn it, lady!" The coach popped out of the chair with astonishing quickness. Mo felt her body tense as she rose out of her chair. The coach sucked air, hands balled at his sides. She watched him struggle for control. She had time to reflect that he had probably been a very good wrestler.

"We all loved Charlie Connell," he said.

"So folks kept it secret."

"Folks kept it secret."

Mo forced herself to take a deep breath, willing herself calm. She felt like apologizing but had no idea what for.

"Now what?" the coach asked.

"Now I keep trying to find out who killed Charlie."

He nodded. His hands were still fisted at his sides.

"I can find my way out."

She didn't turn to look back until she was in the hall. The coach was leaning forward, fists on the desk, head down.

As she walked swiftly away, relief flooded her, and she realized how frightened she'd been.

Folks put their lawn chairs out at dawn to stake out prime positions. They brought their six packs, thermoses, and flasks, and a few even hauled out the barbecues for a little sidewalk grilling. Radio Station WYUU set up its remote unit on the corner in front of Charlie's, and Ronnie Modrell prepared to describe the proceedings.

The weather gave the Annual Mitchell Volunteer Firemen's Parade its blessing, conferring sunny skies, puffy white clouds, and mild temperatures—the kind of day folks in the upper Midwest endure six months of winter to get to, the kind of day old people put off dying to see one more of, the kind that breaks your heart with its beauty.

"Can't last," they said.

"We'll pay for it later."

"If the farmers don't get some rain, we'll be in a pretty pickle."

The fire truck came first, of course.

The smoke-eaters hung off the sides of the old pumper, tossing candy. The kids scurried after the Tootsie Rolls and Sweet Tarts that skittered across the pavement.

When the truck pulled even with the diner, the chief let the siren wail. The kids screamed and clapped their hands over their ears, dogs howled, and the grown-ups cheered and clapped.

And some of them cried.

Then came the Adamskis in their pink 1957 T-Bird convertible. Harold wore his tuxedo, Martha her blue taffeta gown.

Next came those members of VFW Post 419 still able to march, with two young Desert Storm vets in among the old timers, and then the Knights of Columbus in their black sashes. The wavy-haired, smiling former television anchorman and current State Representative jogged back and forth across the street, handing candy to the kiddies and literature to any adult who would take it. The Shriners in their clown outfits, riding in their miniature cars and bouncing on their crazy bikes, tooted and snorted and pelted the kids with still more candy.

As soon as the flatbed truck pulled by Eddie McCafferty's ancient John Deere tractor brought the State Champion Class D Girls Basketball Squad within range of the boys lining the roof of Charlie's, they opened fire with water balloons and squirt guns. The State Champs retaliated with water balloons of their own, propelled by a wicked rubber sling that generated impressive force.

When the water carnage subsided, the equestrian unit picked its way past the crowd, horses sagging under bulky riders and fancy saddles.

The Mitchell Soon to be Not Very Famous Non Marching Band rolled through on another flatbed truck, rendering their signature song, the "In Heaven There is No Beer" polka.

The parade's one float and last unit turned the corner and rattled onto Main. The little wooden playhouse perched on Elmo Valler's wagon, swaying precariously, with Charlie's Angels hanging on the sides.

The crowd got real quiet. "Charlie would have loved this," Ronnie Modrell said into his microphone. "He would have been real proud to see this." Then even Ronnie Modrell got quiet.

The Haslett's border collie started barking several blocks away.

Elmo braked, and Sabra stepped down.

"Charlie," she said, looking up at the endless blue sky. "If you can hear us, this one's for you."

The bandwagon had gone around the block and come up behind the diner float. Lester Bannon gave the downbeat, and they began to play a jagged "Limelighter Blues," a particular favorite of Charlie's.

Peter Detrick, head of the local VFW, came forward, his hands wrapped tightly around the flagpole wedged into a leather pouch at his waist. Men doffed their seed caps. Women shushed their children. Freddie Johnson drummed a roll as best he knew to do, and Johnny "Waco" Reilly blew the first several bars of The National Anthem on his trumpet. The rest of the band came in softly on the rockets red glare.

As the last notes faded, Freida Taggert flipped the switch at the Methodist Church, unleashing the recorded church bells that signal noon in Mitchell every weekday.

The Parade was over.

Folks lingered, and many started walking out to Fireman's Park, where the carnival rides, food booths, and craft fair were already open, and the Mitchell Marauders Post 13 American Legion team would take on the Cashton Crushers at 1:00.

Mo decided to go to the office and develop her film of the parade for the two-page photo spread she planned for Thursday's edition. Then she might go to the park for awhile. There was no reason to hurry home to an empty house.

In the darkroom, the faces of the townspeople emerged in the clear chemical wash, like ghosts rematerializing. She had written of their births and marriages and deaths, tracked their comings and goings, tried to make sense of their politics. She had gotten to know many of them. She called a few of them friend. But since Charlie's death, she caught herself wondering if she really knew them and the town at all.

As she watched the faces emerge from shadows, she wondered if she were seeing the face of a killer among them.

The phone rang. She considered letting it ring, but she had no talent for such things. She took the print out of the tray, squeegeed off the moisture, hung it, and wiped her hands on her apron. She slid through the curtain and caught the phone in mid-ring.

"*Doings*. This is Mo."

"Hey?"

"You're home!"

"I just got in. How was the parade?"

"Read all about it in Thursday's edition."

"Are you still mad?"

She took a steadying breath. "No," she said. "I worked through that after you called last night."

"I am sorry. You just can't plan when your teenage son will decide to confide in you. By the time I got him home, it was too late to drive back."

"So you had to sleep over."

"Come on, Mo."

"You didn't sleep at Claudia's?"

"I slept on the couch. Downstairs. With my clothes on."

"I'm sure you defended your virtue."

"You're better than this."

"Not right now."

"Why don't you come home, and we'll salvage what's left of the holiday? Maybe we can come back to town for the fireworks later."

"We could do that. I've got one more roll to develop."

"Good. I'll see you in about an hour, then."

She chided herself as she hung up and went back into the darkroom. The thought of Claudia still being involved in Doug's life twisted her stomach into a tight knot.

She took down the last print she had developed and held it up in the red safe light. She had shot it from in front of the Hair Apparent, catching Sabra, the float, and the diner in the background. She stared intently at the picture, as if something in it could tell her how Charlie had died.

If there were a clue in the picture, Mo couldn't find it.

"We got the guy who killed Charlie."

Mo put her hand over the receiver and hissed "Repoz" to Doug, who was sitting beside her on the couch.

They had been listening to Dvorak's Ninth, from the New World Symphony. Doug picked up the remote and hit pause.

"We can put this kid with Charlie the night of the murder," the sheriff continued. "We've got motive, and we've got opportunity. We've got our killer."

"A kid, you said?"

Doug was watching her, a concerned look on his face.

"Seventeen years old. Makes you sick, doesn't it?"

"Who is it?" Mo felt her gut tighten.

"Name's Marcus Trevin. He's a senior at the high school."

"I interviewed him once. Does Myers have this yet?"

"Nope. I told you I'd give you a head start."

"Thanks. Have you charged him?"

"Not yet. We have until tomorrow."

And then Myers would be all over it, Mo thought, Myers

and every other reporter from Sheboygan to the Mississippi River. And she didn't go to press for two more days. So much for her head start.

Then she felt ashamed for thinking of the story ahead of poor Marcus and his family.

"We got three guys who put this Trevin kid at the VFW Hall with Charlie that night," Repoz said. "And two more saw him walking off with Charlie afterwards. And this Wildman character, the guy who owns the video rental place, puts somebody who matches Trevin's description outside the diner arguing with Charlie."

"What does Marcus say?"

"He says he was with his lady friend all night. One… hold on…"

She could hear him flipping through his notebook. Reporters and cops were a lot alike, she reflected, always scribbling things in notebooks and then hunting for them later.

"Here we go. Kramer. Cindy Kramer. She backs his story, of course. But nobody saw them together, and Trevin's account of the evening doesn't square with hers."

"But why would Marcus kill Charlie?"

"That part gets a little seamy."

"Go on."

"Charlie had himself a little problem. A sex problem. An unnatural attraction for young people of the same sex, shall we say? We figure Charlie was trying to get over on this Trevin kid, but Trevin wasn't having any. That's what they were arguing about."

"But that was at 10:00. Charlie didn't die until at least two hours later."

"We figure Trevin either came back on his own, or Charlie lured him back one way or another. Charlie wouldn't take 'no' for an answer, they fought, and Marcus killed him. Did I mention he's a wrestler? He's not a big kid, but he's strong and in shape. He wouldn't have had any trouble handling Charlie."

Mo felt as if she might be sick. Beyond that, something didn't feel right.

"The kid's never even gotten a tardy slip," Repoz said. "An honor student. Even so, the DA will want to push this into adult court, given the ugly mood the public's in."

"He has an attorney?"

"Oh, yeah. The family attorney. Big Madison law firm. And his coach is here, too."

"His coach?"

"Yeah. I got his name right here. Norbert Hopkins. What kind of name is Norbert?"

"Probably named for the saint. Why did you pull him in?"

"We didn't. He came in on his own. Says he wants us to go easy on the boy. He also says this wasn't the first time Charlie tried to put the moves on one of his boys. But that doesn't come as news to you. Am I right?"

Mo felt a ripple of apprehension. "Hopkins might have mentioned something about that," she said. "Off the record, of course."

"Of course. And that's why you didn't report it to me?"

Mo's mind raced through the trouble she might be in.

"Although, as I understand it, 'off the record' doesn't mean you can't tell the authorities something that might have bearing on a murder case. It's not like with a priest and confessions. Right?"

"Right." Mo had to push the word up through a suddenly tight throat.

"You were just protecting your source. Right?"

"I was researching a profile. That wasn't the sort of material I could use."

Doug moved in close. Mo held the phone an inch from her ear so Doug could hear.

"You didn't think this might be something I should know about?"

"I really didn't think I had anything to report."

Mo had gotten over being frightened and was starting to be angry. The Sheriff was bullying her, trying to get her to grovel. No way, she thought. If he wants to throw me in jail, let him do it.

"You know," Repoz said, "it occurs to me that you might have been holding out on me. Maybe hoping to solve the crime before I did."

"Sheriff, I didn't know anything about Marcus Trevin talking with Charlie the night of the murder."

"Still, you did know about Charlie's problem. Maybe you and me need to have a little chat about withholding evidence."

"Fine."

"Meanwhile, why don't you just steer clear of this mess until we get it all wrapped up. When I've got something for you, I'll let you know. Are we straight on that?"

"Absolutely."

"Glad to hear it. Good night now."

The line went dead.

"That little creep!" She turned to her husband. "They've got a high school kid in custody for Charlie's murder. They haven't charged him yet, but they're going to. His coach is trying to get them to go easy on him. Repoz says the DA will want to try him as an adult."

"What was that other stuff, about you holding out?"

"You heard the man."

"Is that serious?"

Mo shook her head. "If he's got his killer, he comes out looking like a genius. He won't give me any grief."

"What if it turns out that this kid didn't do it?"

"Do you think he's innocent?"

"I don't know, but you think so."

"And you put no stock in intuition." She took a deep breath. "You're right. I don't. It just doesn't add up."

"Do the math for me."

"Coach Hopkins told me about Charlie's previous attempt to put the make on one of his wrestlers, but he didn't mention the more recent occurrence with Marcus. Why not?"

"That's easy. He was protecting the kid from a murder rap."

"Right. So why didn't he protect him from Repoz, the one who's vote really counts?"

"That's easy, too. Withholding information from a newspaper editor isn't a crime."

"Good point. But Hopkins volunteered the information to the sheriff. He didn't even wait to be asked."

Doug shrugged. "Maybe he figured they'd have come looking for him soon enough, and he'd look better by coming forward."

"Maybe." Mo picked up the remote and jiggled it in her hand.

"You've got a feeling, right?"

She gave him The Look.

"I wasn't patronizing you!"

She laughed, but her smile faded immediately. "I've talked with Marcus Trevin. He's a decent kid, Doug. He can look an adult in the eye and carry on a conversation. Most of them can't."

"That doesn't mean he didn't kill Charlie."

"But look. Charlie argued with somebody outside the diner the night he was murdered. The description fits Marcus Trevin, which proves nothing. The description also fits Pete the dishwasher and lots of other people. But let's say it was Marcus."

"Okay. Let's say that."

"Why did he leave and then come back later?"

Doug reached out and idly stroked Mo's bare arm. Mo shook her head. "I've talked with Norb Hopkins twice now," she said, "and both times, I got the feeling something wasn't right about him."

"You just be sure you steer clear of him," Doug said, putting his arm around her and drawing her close.

"That's just what Repoz said. 'Steer clear.' And let a nice kid take the fall for a murder he didn't commit."

"*Maybe* didn't commit."

"Maybe didn't commit."

"And maybe take the fall. Who knows what will happen at the trial?"

She rolled into his embrace. "Repoz needed a quick collar. I'm not so sure he cares if he's got the right guy or not."

Doug sighed. "You're not going to let go of this, are you?" he asked.

"No," she said. "Not until I'm sure."

Would the DA seek to try the defendant as an adult, Myers of the *Cardinal-Herald* wanted to know the following afternoon at the press conference announcing the arrest of Marcus Trevin for the murder of Charlie Connell.

Given the severity of the crime and the youth's age—he would be turning 18 in less than two months—that seemed likely, yes, according to the Sheriff.

Would they seek murder one? Myers again.

Too early to tell, the Sheriff allowed.

"The little fart really redeemed himself with a quick arrest," Myers muttered as the reporters herded out of the hearing room and raced for the telephones.

Yeah, Mo thought, if he has the right guy.

Marcus Trevin will go to jail to await a hearing to set bail, if any, and his family will plunge into the stoic mourning that is part shame and part defiance, Mo reflected on the drive back to Mitchell.

And we'll all realize how much Charlie meant to the town, she thought. Some things would get done without him, but they would all have to learn to get along without the rest.

Life would go on. The School Board and the County Council would keep squabbling, and Mo would keep writing about it. The mosquitoes would keep biting, and cicadas would still provide the soundtrack for a midwestern summer.

The diner seemed empty and forlorn as she drove by, despite all the plants and flowers folks had been putting on the doorstep out front.

A young woman jumped up from the chair by the window as soon as Mo walked into the *Doings* office.

"Is that her?" she asked Vi.

"She's been waiting almost an hour," Vi told Mo. "She says it's urgent."

"You have to help me!" the woman said.

"That's okay, Vi." Mo turned toward the young lady, who was small, blonde, and just short of hysterical.

"Let's talk in the other room," Mo said.

She put her hand gently on the woman's elbow and led her into the back, closing the door behind them.

"Can I get you something? I've got coffee or juice."

She shook her head, whipping the air with her blonde ponytail. She took the straight-backed metal chair Mo offered. Mo took another chair and faced her. "Mo Quinn," she said, holding out a hand.

"I'm Cindy. Kramer. You have to help him. He didn't kill that awful man."

"Are we talking about Marcus?"

"He was with me. They won't believe me. They think I'm just saying that to protect him."

"I'm going to get some coffee. You sure you don't want anything?"

"No, thank you."

Mo filled a Styrofoam cup with coffee from the stained pot on the hot plate and brought it and a couple of paper napkins back to the chair. She handed Cindy the napkins, and Cindy dabbed at her eyes.

"What time was Marcus with you?"

"When they say he killed that man."

"What time was that?"

"I'm not sure."

"It's important."

"Late. He'd been meeting with that committee. He was the representative from the high school."

Mo gently drew out the story. They didn't really have a date, because of the meeting, but Marcus came to her house afterwards. He was very upset. She let him into the house—her parents were at a play in Madison—and he told her 'that man' had tried to do something horrible to him.

"He was practically crying," Cindy said, tears staining her face.

"Charlie Connell asked him to perform oral sex on him."

Cindy nodded, her eyes averted.

"And Marcus refused."

"Of course!" Her head snapped up, and her eyes met Mo's. "It's disgusting!"

Mo put a hand gently on Cindy's arm. Cindy snuffled and blew her nose loudly into one of the napkins.

"Did anyone see you together that night?"

"He didn't kill that man! He would never do a thing like that. You have to believe me."

"I do."

"The Sheriff doesn't."

"Nobody saw Marcus with you."

She shook her head miserably.

"How long did he stay?"

Cindy shrugged. "About an hour," she said. "We just talked. Then I said he'd better go, because my parents would be coming home, and I'm not supposed to have him over when they're not there. They're very strict."

"What time did he leave?"

"I don't know."

"About what time?"

"Maybe midnight."

"Do you know if Marcus went straight home?"

"I don't know. I don't think so."

"What makes you say that?"

She shrugged. "He wouldn't have wanted to go home."

"Where else would he go?"

She shook her head.

"If you tell me, I might be able to help."

"He might have gone to see the coach."

"Coach Hopkins?"

She nodded. "He didn't get along very well with his father. Coach Hopkins was like a father figure to him. Can you help him?"

"I don't know," Mo admitted. "But I do know this. I don't think we know the truth of this yet, and I'm going to keep looking."

"What can I do?"

"You be there for Marcus. He needs you and your faith in him very much."

"I will." She nodded resolutely, and Mo saw strength mixed with youth and confusion and fear in her eyes.

"I know you will," Mo said, gripping her hand.

. . . .

Half the town made the drive to Madison for the arraignment, creating a grim parody of the trek they would make for a state high school football or basketball tournament.

Mo watched with a dull ache in her breast as Marcus Trevin sat at the defendant's table, looking small and vulnerable in his new suit.

Cindy Kramer was among those in the gallery, of course, as was Coach Hopkins, who looked grim. The crowd seemed to sigh when the assistant DA announced her intention to seek murder in the first degree, based on the fact that the defendant had left the scene and come back, thereby clearly establishing premeditation.

The defense will hammer at the sordid details of Charlie's past, Mo figured on the drive back. They'll stress the lack of evidence putting Marcus back at the diner the second time. All they have to do is create reasonable doubt.

But a counter theory wouldn't hurt, and nobody seemed to have come up with another suspect to replace Marcus.

She should do something fun with Doug this weekend, she decided. They hadn't had any time together in weeks, except for the fractured Fourth of July. He had a softball game Saturday—he played third base for the Senile Dementia, a men's fast-pitch softball team in the county recreation league. Maybe she should go to the game to watch him. They could go canoeing afterwards.

She slowed as she approached the town. The sight of the closed diner again brought a pang of grief, for Charlie, for the town, and now for Marcus and Cindy and their families.

As she braked for the stop sign at the corners, she thought she saw someone or something disappear around the corner of the diner. At the same time, she remembered something that had been nagging her from some corner of her subconscious since she interviewed Bill Heiss at the Museum.

She turned at the corner and drove around to park at the back of the diner, out of sight of the road. Somewhere in that diner she would find the clue that would enable her to figure out who really killed Charlie. She was sure of it. She didn't know why she felt this way, and she didn't know what the clue was, but it would be there, in the subbasement she had learned about but hadn't investigated. She was willing to bet the Sheriff hadn't investigated it, either, probably didn't even know about it.

The back door was locked, but the basement window to the right of the door had been broken. Mo got a rag from the trunk of the car and wrapped it around her left hand. She picked up a rock and broke out the rest of the glass. She was able to slip her hand in and unlatch the window, which swung up and out.

Mo got on her knees and peered inside. There was nothing on the floor, just a short drop from the window. She went in head first, rolling onto the concrete floor. She sat for a moment, her legs drawn up to her chest, to catch her breath and let her eyes adjust to the dark. The basement was cool even in the heat of the day, with the dank, dark smell of decay. She saw the single bed, sheets and blankets still piled on top, and a writing table, bookshelf, and cabinet. From the way things looked, Charlie might have been right upstairs, serving up his wonderful omelets.

But he wasn't serving omelets. He was dead, and he had died right here. Mo's shiver wasn't from the dampness and cold.

She inched cautiously across the narrow room to the stairway leading up to the diner. Something was missing, but she couldn't decide what.

Other than the locked door behind her and the window

she had tumbled through, there didn't appear to be any other way in or out of the basement. If I had a subbasement to store my beer, Mo pondered, where would I put it?

She began feeling her way along the wall. She was almost directly across the room from the stairway when she heard the door at the top of the stairs open. Light knifed into the room like pain as she crouched down.

"Who's in here?" a voice called out.

Mo released the breath she hadn't realized she was holding.

"Dilly? It's okay. It's me."

"Mokwin. What are you doing here?"

Mo got up slowly. "You scared me!" she admitted.

"I'm sorry. I come here every day. I keep things clean."

That's what was missing—the dust and cobwebs that should have reclaimed the narrow cell by now.

"Whatcher looking for, Mokwin?"

"Do you know if there's another part to the basement? Another room?"

Dilly's face clouded. Then he brightened. "The place that smells like beer!"

"Yes!" Mo almost shouted. "That's it. Where is it?"

"Charlie didn't want me to go there. He kept his things there."

"Things?"

"Secret things."

"It's okay now, Dilly. I'm with you."

"Nobody knows about it but me. It was Charlie's secret place, but I knew about it. He didn't want me to go there."

"Would you show it to me?"

"Sure I will."

"Thank you, Dilly."

Mo followed Dilly up the stairs into the diner, which was as clean as the day Charlie closed it for the last time, the counters and floor spotless in the dim light from the street.

"You've kept it very nice," Mo said.

"Yes," Dilly said, nodding.

He went around the counter and into the kitchen. Mo glanced out the front window to make sure they weren't being observed before following him. Frowning, she crossed the kitchen and peered into the storage closet. Dilly had disappeared.

"Hello?" she called out, feeling foolish as she walked around the kitchen.

"Boo! I fooled you!"

A startled yelp escaped her. She whirled to see Dilly grinning in the closet doorway.

"How did you do that?"

"Come here! I'll show you."

This time she hurried to keep Dilly in sight. He stood by the shelf that comprised the back wall of the narrow storage area. "Lookit!" he said. Grinning, he turned and shoved on the corner of the shelf. It slid open, revealing a staircase.

Dilly took a flashlight off the shelf and handed it to her. "It's dark. I don't clean down here. I don't like it."

Heart pounding with fear and anticipation, she followed Dilly down the stairs into a wide, deep chamber. A yeasty, beery smell seemed to permeate the walls and floor.

"I threw the picture books away," Dilly said. "Did I do wrong?"

Dilly's face looked small and frightened in the halo of light from the flashlight.

"What picture books?"

"Charlie's. They made me feel bad to look at them. I threw them away."

"No, Dilly. You didn't do wrong. Charlie wouldn't have wanted anyone to see them."

She shone the flashlight around the cavern. A couple of old chairs, a bed or sofa, and heaps of pillows crowded one corner. The room seemed to be empty otherwise. By the far wall, something had obviously been cemented over, probably the entrance to a ramp to move the beer in and out.

Something crunched beneath her sneaker. She knelt down, shining the light on the floor. She scooped up a handful of…what? Peanut shells?

When she realized what she held in her hand, she wanted to throw them down. Instead she dug a handkerchief out of her jeans pocket, carefully wrapped the husks, and thrust them into the pocket.

"I'm sorry," Dilly said. "I don't clean here."

"That's all right." Mo put a hand gently on his shoulder. "I'm glad you didn't."

She shuffled cautiously across the room. Her foot brushed something. She bent down and peered at the strangely shaped brown bottle revealed in the circle of light. Gingerly, she picked up the bottle by the end of the neck.

"Can we go now? I don't like this place," Dilly whined.

"I don't like it either. But I'm really glad you showed it to me."

Suddenly she realized that she wanted very badly to get out, too. Quickly she led Dilly back up the steps to daylight.

She called the Sheriff from the *Doings* office. Sheriff Repoz "wasn't available," and she didn't want to trust what she had to anyone else.

She broke the connection and hit the speed dial for her home line but got her own voice on the recorder. She tried Doug's business line, but it rang through to voice mail, too.

Panic tried to well up in her. Tuesday afternoon had become Tuesday evening, and she had to get the paper ready for the printer. She longed to rip up the front page and run the biggest story in the history of the *Doings*, but she didn't have enough yet, and she couldn't hold the paper until she did.

Everyone in town would have known she'd be at the *Doings* working late on a Tuesday night. Lots of folks relied on it, in fact, bringing in last minute notices of club meetings and church dinners. At first Doug had worried about her being there alone at night. He'd even "dropped by" a few times, to make sure she was okay. Touched, but also somewhat annoyed by his hovering, she'd put him to work, and Doug had proved to be a pretty fair hand at cranking out a two-column, two-line headline.

She could have used his company and his help this night, but he was practicing with the Senile Dementia.

Joanne Christensen dropped off her copy for the library book sale—a barely decipherable scrawl on lined paper.

Mo worked at the computer in the back room, trying to slice a couple of paragraphs off her lengthy county council story to make room for the library notice. She found no easy cuts, so she had to go through, word by word.

She sat in the glow from the screen, darkness gathering around her without her noticing.

She heard the front door click shut.

Dilly? Doug? Her heartbeat accelerated, and the fuzz at the nape of her neck bristled. She sat perfectly still, hands poised above the keyboard.

A floorboard creaked.

"Back here," she called out, trying to sound calm.

She stared at the doorway. When the bulky form of Coach Hopkins filled it, she felt at once surprised and confirmed.

"You startled me."

"Didn't mean to."

"What can I do for you?"

"We have to move the day for the wrestling team orientation meeting. I was hoping you could get something in the paper. If it's not too late."

"Sure. No problem."

The coach handed over the single sheet. Mo stuck it on her typing rack. She turned back to the screen, the coach standing to her left.

"Was there something else?" She risked a glance.

The coach pulled a small cellophane bag from his shirt pocket and, tilting his head back, emptied some of the contents into his mouth. "Been hooked on these darn things since I gave up tobacco," he said.

Mo continued to type but had no idea what she was writing. She scanned the table and floor for something she could use as a weapon. She covered by grabbing the metal wastebasket and shoving it toward him. The coach leaned over and spit husks into the wastebasket.

"Shame about Marcus," he said. "Who would have thought a boy like that could do such a thing? I guess you never know, huh?"

The computer table was at the far end of the narrow room. Coach Hopkins had the door blocked. The AP Style Manual seemed to be the only potential weapon within reach. She might be able to do some damage with the spiral binding.

"I guess a jury will have to sort it out," she said, watching him.

"He must of done it, though, don't you think? I mean, who else could it of been?" The coach leaned to spit again, spraying half the husks onto the floor. "Sorry," he said, wiping spittle from his chin.

"No problem," Mo said again, hating how squeaky her voice sounded. Her heart was pounding, and her mind was circling in ever-tighter spirals.

"I ran into Dilly awhile ago."

"Did you?"

"Yeah. He said the two of you had been poking around at Charlie's."

"He showed me how clean he's been keeping everything."

"Yeah. He show you that hideaway place Charlie had?"

"What place is that?"

His eyes were intent, calculating. He was trying to figure out what she knew, Mo realized.

"They'll probably go pretty easy on Marcus, don't you think?" the coach said. "On account of the circumstances, and him being so young and all. Don't you figure?"

Another splattering of seeds. His mouth held a lot of seeds. A laugh bubbled up in her. She fought it down.

This is no time to panic, girl, she told herself.

On the contrary, she answered herself. This is the perfect time to panic!

Would a scream reach the street? Would anyone be there to hear it?

His slab hands squeezed each other. He took a step forward. He was very close now. His face was partially illuminated by the computer screen.

The phone started ringing in the other room.

"Leave it," he said.

They waited until the phone rang itself out.

"When did you figure it out?" His voice was offhand, almost pleasant.

"Figure what out?"

She inched the chair away from the desk, trying to give herself space to stand up. The chair cut the backs of her legs.

"I'm real sorry about all this," he said. "But you see how things are. I don't know what the hell else I can do."

"You can't get away with it."

It was bad enough to have to die, she chided herself, without spouting trite movie dialogue for your last words.

"Maybe. Maybe not. But I can't let you go, can I? Not with what you know."

"You were in a rage," Mo said, slowly standing. "It wasn't premeditated. Marcus came to you for help. You went a little bit crazy. Wasn't that the way it was? But if you kill me, that's deliberate, planned. Don't you see how much worse that makes things?"

"Nope. Not really."

It occurred to Mo that Coach Hopkins was beyond reasoning. With the thought came a ball of cold, sick dread deep in her guts.

"Everybody loved Charlie," he said, his face darkening into a scowl. "They didn't know what he really was." He was wringing his hands again, as if trying to squeeze his rage out through the tips of his fingers. "They should have put him away someplace." The light had gone out of his eyes.

"A jury would understand that."

"I can't take that chance. They'll go easy on Marcus."

The screen saver snapped on, so that the only light came from the doorway behind the coach. He glanced at the darkened screen. In that instant, she brought her knee up. The coach grunted with pain and surprise. Mo shoved him with both hands. She tried to slip past him, but he grabbed her shoulders hard, sending a bolt of pain down her arms.

A growl escaped her. Her left arm shot up, palm out, hitting his mouth solidly and sliding up to shove his nose hard into his skull. He let out a howl of pain, his hands slipping from her shoulders. She shoved past him and out into the front room. The coach was in the doorway behind her, blood spurting from his nose, his eyes dull with pain and hate.

As she watched, his legs seemed to dissolve under him. He buckled and pitched forward, hitting the floor face first.

Mo stood, panting. She felt something wet and sticky on her face, reached up, and brought away a bloody hand. She began to shake, cold spreading from her spine into her shoulders and arms. Her knees turned to water. She groped and fell backward into Vi's chair. The chair swiveled with her weight, so she was facing the window. As if in a dream, she saw Doug running up the street toward her, just before she lost consciousness.

# 21

Cora Beth Watkins wore a flower-pattern dress with pastel blues, yellows and reds. Minnie had obviously been bathed, brushed, and blown dry, and sported a huge pink bow.

"You hold Minnie," Cora Beth insisted to Pete when Mo posed them in front of the quilt Cora Beth had hanging in the dining room. Pete held his hands out, and Minnie squirmed into his arms, looked up at Pete, and licked his chin just as Mo tripped the shutter. Mo would run the picture over four columns on the front page. It was that good.

"I wish I could give you more than just cookies," Cora Beth said as she passed the plate of her specialty treats. "If I only had money…"

"He'll be earning his own money again," Mo assured her. "Andy Krueger is going to reopen the diner, and he's going to hire Pete to take care of cleanup."

"He might even give me a shot at the grill," Pete said, ducking his head.

"That's wonderful!" Cora Beth said.

"And Charlene Connell has agreed to bake her pies again," Mo added, splurging on a fat cookie dripping with chocolate.

Mo got back from dropping Pete off at his trailer late that afternoon. Doug had dinner ready but was quiet as they ate out on the porch. He went to his office as soon as they finished, leaving Mo to do the dishes. After she finished cleaning up, she proofed copy out on the porch, watching the bees flit among the flowers and listening to an owl in the nearby woods. But his silence called her inside. He'd been quiet since that night at the *Doings* when she had fought off Coach Hopkins. She guessed he was upset with her for putting herself in danger, but his mood was going on too long.

The Associated Press had picked up Mo's account of the arrest of Norb Hopkins, and she was still getting clips from newspapers all over the country. A producer had spotted the story, and they had actually flown Mo to Chicago to be interviewed on Oprah.

Doug had seemed happy with her sudden celebrity. But could he be a little bit jealous? Did he feel somehow inadequate?

She found him at his computer. She stood behind him, massaging his shoulders.

"What are you working on?"

"I'm analyzing the other four trades between Harry Frazee and the Yankees."

"The way you say that, I'm pretty sure I'm supposed to know about the fifth one."

"Frazee sold Babe Ruth to the Yankees, thus inflicting the famous 'Curse of the Bambino' on the Red Sox."

"I thought Babe Ruth was born a Yankee."

"Nope. He was a pitcher for the Sox first. Frazee sold

him for $50,000. He'd had a series of flops on Broadway and needed the money."

"He was a pitcher?"

"One of the best." Doug swiveled in his chair to look up at her. "I'm hoping to publish this in the *SABR Journal*. Will you look it over for me, when I've got it in shape?"

"I'd love to."

He took her hand gently and pulled her into his lap. "Then I couldn't hope for a better editor," he said. He was smiling, but his voice was serious. "The woman who broke the heartland murder story."

"It must have been a slow news day," she said, snuggling against him.

"It was a great story."

"Thanks."

"But from now on, I hope you'll just write the news instead of making it."

"Amen to that. Tell me something."

"Anything, dear heart."

"How is it that you happened to be coming to the office just then? I thought you had softball practice."

"You had the situation well in hand by the time I got there."

"Not if Hopkins had come to before I could get help. But you didn't answer my question."

"Since when do I need a reason to visit?"

"You don't. I was just wondering if you had sensed that I needed help."

He smiled. "You think I might have had one of those intuitions, huh?" His face became serious. "God, Mo. When I think of what could have happened…"

She kissed him. The chair pitched forward, and they almost fell out.

"Let's slip into something more stable," she suggested, laughing. "Something flat and low to the ground."

They walked upstairs side by side and undressed each other slowly, lovingly. He caressed and kissed her neck and shoulders, and they slid naturally into making love.

"So, tell me," he said afterwards, as they held hands under the light sheet that was their only covering on a warm summer night. "When did you get it all figured out?"

"On our honeymoon, love."

"Not that. I mean Charlie."

"You know I was suspicious from the get-go."

"Because of those aprons hanging on their hooks."

"Yep. And the strange mark on Charlie's forehead bothered me, too. How could he have gotten that from falling down the stairs?"

"He did he get it?"

"Hopkins skulled him with one of the old beer bottles down in the subbasement. It had a raised emblem on it."

"But that still wouldn't have pointed you at Hopkins."

"You're right. Even though I was suspicious of him, I didn't really put it together until Cindy Kramer told me she thought Marcus might have gone to see his coach that night. Then I found the sunflower seed husks in the subbasement. That clinched it."

"I guess when Hopkins tried to kill you, you had that second-source confirmation you always say you need, right?"

"You have been paying attention! I just don't understand why I didn't figure it out sooner. I just assumed the short man in the stocking cap was Pete, and that threw me off. Repoz found out it was Marcus and assumed he was also the murderer."

"But Marcus ran to his coach, and it was the coach who came gunning for Charlie."

"Hopkins would have had a mad brewing ever since Charlie exposed himself to one of his 'kids' years ago. And he must have known about the subbasement from that episode. So he took Charlie down there to kill him where nobody would hear."

"And then tried to make it look like an accident."

"Yep. And almost got away with it, too."

"Quite a little imbroglio."

"Wasn't he the guy the Cubs traded Lou Brock for?"

Doug laughed.

Hopkins says he never meant to kill Charlie," Mo continued.

"He would have killed you, too. Don't forget that."

"He was desperate."

"Are you defending him?"

"Trying to understand him, I guess. In his way, he's done a lot of good for a lot of kids in this town. Including Marcus."

"Is that why Marcus was willing to take the fall for the murder?"

"Loyalty, maybe. Don't coaches inspire that sort of thing?"

"I've heard of taking one for the team, but that's pretty extreme."

"He might have felt guilty, too. He might have figured he did something to make Charlie come on to him. And if he hadn't told the coach, Charlie would still be alive."

"That's true."

Doug stroked her arm. They were quiet. Doug's breathing slowed, but Mo knew he wasn't asleep yet.

"Dougie?"

"Hmmm?"

"Are you absolutely sure you didn't have maybe the teensiest intuition that I needed you that night?"

"I did feel a little twinge," he said after awhile, a smile in his voice.

"I knew it!"

"I think it might be a touch of bursitis."

"Oh, you."

"Mo?"

"Yeah."

"I love you more than my life. The thought of losing you scares the hell out of me."

"Don't worry. No more Nancy Drew. I promise. Being married to the man of my dreams is excitement enough."

She couldn't know, of course, that in just two months Mitchell's beloved parish priest would be brutally murdered, plunging her into another murder investigation.

For now, she felt safe and warm in her husband's arms.

 **COMING SOON:
A brand new Monona Quinn
mystery by Marshall Cook!**

Visit www.diversityincorporated.com, where you can
find more information on this and other releases from
Bleak House Books, read an interview with author Marshall
Cook, and browse the complete catalog of books available
from Diversity, Inc.

An excerpt from the next Monona Quinn mystery:

The headlights illuminate the statue of the Virgin Mary on her pedestal as the sedan crawls to a stop a few feet from the entrance of St. Anne's Catholic Church. The passenger side door clicks open, releasing a small pool of light. Debussy's "La Mer" spills into the warm night. A small man wearing black pants and shirt and a white clerical collar emerges.

"Are you sure you won't come in for a nightcap?" he says, leaning down to address the driver, a thickset man also yoked with the collar of the priesthood.

"It's late, James," the driver says loudly, as one does to the hard of hearing or those whose English is poor. "I have promises to keep."

"And miles to go before you sleep."

"Yes. And miles to go before I sleep."

The inside car light illuminates the two faces. The little man straightens up, gives his shirt an unnecessary tug, and closes the door with a solid thump.

"Good night, then," he says.

The sedan pulls away. The priest stands, his right hand raised as if in benediction. The car bellies through the gully and turns onto the highway heading away from town. The priest slowly mounts the steps of the church, the heels of his black loafers clicking on the concrete. He pauses to peer up into the serene face of the blessed mother. Behind her, the church is dark, the tall cross on the spire thrusting toward the distant, unblinking stars.

"Hail, Mary, full of grace," the priest murmurs softly. "The Lord is with thee."

A breeze stirs the leaves in the oaks looming over the church.

The priest puts a hand on the pedestal, pats it. "Sweet

mother of mercy," he says, "pray for us, that we may be made worthy of the promises of Christ."

He walks the few steps to the church, grasps the handles of the heavy wooden double doors and pulls.

"Tight as a tick," he tells the night.

He shuffles around the far side of the church, where the little cemetery stretches down a gentle slope to the highway. The graves nearest the church run parallel with the highway. He can't read the tombstones in the dark, of course, but he knows all the names: Schumacher, Grossman, Krueger, Voght, Schmidt. Beyond these, running perpendicular to the highway, a smaller number of tombstones mark the resting places of Fitzgerald, Flanagan, O'Malley and Donegal.

The priest threads the narrow dirt path to the rectory. Mrs. Dudley has left the light on over the door for him.

He fishes the heavy ring of keys from his trouser pocket, fingers the door key and shakes it free of the others. He inserts the key and rams the door with his shoulder, but it holds fast. He twists the key again and rams harder. The door pops open, nearly throwing him into the entry hall. Silently he enters the house. The door closes behind him with a soft click. The door bolt slides into place with a sharp click. The light above the door vanishes, darkness rushing to replace it.

A man steps from the shadows. He stands motionless until the light from the window at the back of the rectory winks out. He walks steadily and without hurry toward the rectory. His arms hang loosely at his sides. His left hand grips the hilt of a long knife, the kind a hunter might use to gut a deer.

## About the Author

Marshall J. Cook is the author of 21 books, including the novels *The Year of the Buffalo* and *Off Season.* He teaches writing for the University of Wisconsin-Madison Division of Continuing Education and edits *Creativity Connection,* a newsletter for writers. He lives in Madison with his wife, Ellen, their attack Schnauzer, Sprecher, and their two Persian cats, Ralph and Norton. They have a son, Jeremiah.